THE SPIDER:
LEGIONS OF MADNESS

THE
MASTER OF MEN!
SPIDER ®

LEGIONS OF MADNESS

By Grant Stockbridge

STEEGER BOOKS • 2020

CHAPTER 1
THE MAN FROM MONTMARTRE

A STRANGE restlessness possessed Wentworth. He had to force himself to remain motionless in the lounge chair which the ever-thoughtful Jenkyns had placed beneath the terrace awning for him. This was no alarm of danger, he assured himself impatiently. It was merely a reflection of his superabundant energy which, for weeks now had found no outlet save in his philanthropies and in the fencing rooms of Trienzi's *salle d'armes.*

The Underworld had been quiet except for the usual round of petty crime, nothing that need again summon into existence the Spider, in which guise Wentworth inflicted swift justice upon outstanding criminals. It had been this quietness which had prompted his fiancée, Nita van Sloan, to suggest a short visit in the Austrian Tyrol, which would be deliriously beautiful now. They were to sail tonight....

Wentworth jerked to his feet and strode out into the brilliant downpour of sunlight, stood rigidly a moment. Then he whipped about, entered the cool dim drawing-room. From the far shadows, a figure clad all in white stepped forward, a full-bearded Sikh who lifted beautifully shaped hands to his turbaned forehead in a low salaam. His manner expressed not so much submission as the reverence a brave man feels for another who is even greater.... Wentworth had not summoned him, but

with the sensitiveness of the East, he had guessed his master's need.

Wentworth nodded jerkily, "The *missie sahib* is at Russek's doing some shopping. She will return here for dinner..." He hesitated. Wasn't this rather ridiculous? There was no need for this fierce bodyguard on crowded Fifth Avenue. He shook his

Everyone in the entire section of the city was mad!

head. He would not argue with his strange restlessness. It had, before this, presaged approaching danger.

"Go thou and guard her, Ram Singh!" His voice was harsh.

Ram Singh took a sharp step forward, "There is… danger, *sahib?*"

Wentworth moved his compact shoulders impatiently. "I know of none… and yet…!"

3

The Sikh's movements became swift. He swept a salaam and backed ceremoniously away. "Thy *karma* and *hers* are one," his voice crackled in the explosive Punjabi of his native hills. "If thy soul feels danger…" He was gone….

And still Wentworth could not be quiet. He paced to his private gymnasium, into which the afternoon sun slanted, selected a Toledo blade from a rack of foils and made a series of dexterous lunges at a small ring suspended from the ceiling by cords. It was a congenial task, yet there was a grimness about his finely chiseled lips and his ears were keenly attuned, waiting for Nita's return. When the door-bell buzzed faintly, he did not wait to rack the foil, nor for his butler, Jenkyns, to answer it, but hurried forward himself. Unconsciously, he hummed lightly beneath his breath, an aria from *Marta*. The grim look was gone and a smile tugged at his mouth corners. All his fears had been groundless then. Nita was back….

HE FLUNG wide the door and instinctively fell back into guard position, the foil half-lifting. For a moment alarm thrilled through him. The man outside the door held an automatic negligently in his right hand and, covering the upper half of his face, was a neat, black mask.

"May I compliment you, *m'sieur*, on your deftness with the foil?" the man asked politely, his words touched with the slight nasal accent of a Frenchman.

Wentworth eyed him quietly, the smile still lingering about his mouth corners. He knew no fear, but his apprehensions for Nita flashed back to him… The danger of his own situation he ignored. That automatic undoubtedly could be fired before he

4

could stab with his foil point, but there would be time for only that one shot before the man fell—and hurried shots frequently miss even at short range. Who should know that better than the Spider, whose life had all too often hinged on such knowledge?

The man with the mask said, "You will not object to my coming in?"

Wentworth stepped back, letting his foil's point drop and, close against the wall, pressed his heel firmly on a certain design in the parquet floor. It was as well to summon assistance. He spoke casually, "I usually prefer to know whom I have the honor of entertaining."

"That makes no trouble at all," the Frenchman assured him. "This mask—" he removed it with a swift gesture—"was merely for effect, you comprehend? I am Jules LeFevre!" He said it with pride, with the air of a man who waits acclaim.

Wentworth concealed a swift flicker of his gray-blue eyes. Well might Jules LeFevre await the shocked surprise that would greet his name! In any circles which had contact, however slight, with European crimes, Jules LeFevre, who had been identified through many years simply as the Man from Montmartre, even to the Sureté of Paris, known as the cleverest of France's shrewd criminals. Wentworth smiled slightly, while his brain raced with the memory of the man's past, with speculation on the purpose of his visit. His sense of peril increased. This man was dangerous.

"From the Montmartre, I believe?" he murmured, his face impassive. "To what do I owe the pleasure of this visit?"

Jules LeFevre laughed lightly, with an obvious enjoyment of Wentworth's manner. *"Ma foi!"* he swore. "I had heard of you, *mon ami,* and what I heard does not do you half of the justice." Wentworth saw that he held the automatic even more negligently than before, but that very carelessness bespoke a skill in its use unusual in European criminals. They preferred, usually, the knife or the garrote....

LeFevre shrugged. *"Alors,* I waste your time." He drew an envelope from his pocket, and with a deft movement of the fingers of that one hand, shook out a long, green ticket of the French Line. "I have here your ticket, *m'sieur,* to Paris. I wish that at midnight you board the *Normandie."*

Wentworth stood motionless, eyeing LeFevre. If this were a lesser man he would be inclined to laughter. His eye corners twinkled. Strange that LeFevre should have selected the same ship on which he and Nita had planned—no, still planned—to sail. He did not underestimate LeFevre, nor the courage which had brought him here. But he was still more amused than angry. His thoughts flicked to Nita for a moment, and he shook his head. With Ram Singh beside her, she was in no danger.

"That is kind of you, LeFevre," he responded graciously. "You will not object if I ask a few questions?"

LeFEVRE WAVED his left hand nonchalantly, steadied the right, which held the automatic. "I will answer one for you first of all. Why do I wish you to leave? *Ma foi,* it is simple. I wish to shift my scene of operations to America. In all America only one man  troubles my soul, though even he only slightly. *Ainsi,* I buy you a ticket to Europe! *Magnifique* of me, is it not?"

"Oh, decidedly," Wentworth murmured, studying the shrewd face of his adversary. "I am flattered that my amateurish efforts at criminology should receive your attention."

"I am certain that you are," LeFevre replied, staring him directly in the eye. "And yet it must be that, for no one could believe these foolish notions the police have sometimes entertained, that you are the Spider."

Wentworth's glance was equally quizzical. "As you say, we waste time. I have only two more questions: first, what do you plan to do in America; second, what's the inducement for my departure?"

LeFevre was slightly contemptuous. "As to the first, not to be rude, *m'sieur,* it is none of your business. As to the second, the inducement is… that I hold your betrothed a hostage. Already—" he glanced at his watch—"my men have had her in their power for some fifteen minutes…."

Wentworth's heart gave a great leap, pounded against his ribs. He must have given some betraying movement for LeFevre retreated a half pace, leveled the automatic a little more obviously. But Wentworth made no move to attack. He settled back on his heels. His uneasiness had been justified. But with Ram Singh beside Nita... His lips tightened and his accent was clipped.

"I have no apprehensions on that score," he said, "but as a safety measure, I shall hold you hostage against her safe return. I'll have to trouble you to drop that weapon."

LeFevre laughed shortly. "And how will you trouble me?"

Wentworth made a slight gesture with his left hand. From the doorway behind LeFevre a man leaped forward. LeFevre's head bobbed; his knees went lax for a moment and Wentworth caught him before he fell. It was over in an instant and LeFevre was fully conscious but unarmed. Behind him stood the man Wentworth had summoned by pressing on the parquet design, a grim-mouthed man in a chauffeur's uniform which was strangely like that of an army officer. There was a gleam of humor in the blue eyes which he had inherited from his Gascon forebears. He had LeFevre's automatic in his left hand, a heavy forty-five in his right.

"Anything else, Major?" he asked quietly.

Wentworth shook his head, his face very stern. "No, you may go, Jackson!"

Jackson wheeled with military precision, marched back through the doorway. He and Wentworth had been soldiers together in the war, Sergeant Jackson and Captain—later Major—Wentworth. Jackson had preferred to continue in the service of the man whom above all others he had learned to respect, rather than to accept the commission offered him in the United States army. LeFevre had rapidly regained his composure. He touched his pointed mustaches with a steady hand. "Allow me to compliment you, *m'sieur,*" he drawled. "Your methods may be a bit on the crude side, but they are quite effective."

WENTWORTH RETORTED shortly, "The Sureté wants you and I shall see that they get you! It so happens that I am crossing on the *Normandie*. You will use the ticket you purchased for me and we will deliver you on the other side. In that way, there will be no troublesome extradition proceedings."

The doorbell buzzed again and Jackson opened it for Nita van Sloan. She had several packages in her arms and she came in swiftly. There was always a lithe grace about her movements, but today there was a special vehemence about her stride, a higher color in her cheeks. She put the packages into Jackson's arms and came toward Wentworth, her chin lifted, her eyes bright with anger.

Behind her, Ram Singh ushered two men through the doorway—patently American gangsters. One of them had a savage knife gash across one cheek. The little finger of his left hand was lashed to the little finger of his friend's right hand and they held those bound fingers very gingerly between them. It was apparent that the slightest wrench on their bonds would cause them agony.

There was a hawkish pride in Ram Singh's dark Sikh face. His hand was on the hilt of a long-bladed parang at his side, a knife he must never draw, according to the custom of his people, unless to draw blood....

9

LeFevre leaped to his feet, filthy French, the language of the *Apache* screaming from him. Nita flushed. Wentworth slapped LeFevre resoundingly across the mouth. The profane flood stopped. The Frenchman's face grew livid.

"For that, *m'sieur*," he croaked hoarsely, "you shall give me satisfaction."

Wentworth shrugged. "Tie him up and hold him, Ram Singh," he ordered coldly. "He goes with us tonight to France. Turn these two animals over to the police."

Nita was at his side, her lovely eyes narrowed in anger. "They tried to kidnap me," she rasped, choking a little, with her fury. "They tried to kidnap me!"

Wentworth took her hand. "They didn't succeed, dear," he reminded. He laughed. "You should be used to being kidnapped by now."

Nita snatched her hand free. Heaven knew she should be accustomed to attacks upon her by enemies who sought to strike at Richard Wentworth through her. It had been tried again and again, sometimes with dire results. She said, in exasperation, "I'm not sailing tonight. I'm going to stay here and see that these beasts get the limit."

Wentworth looked at her with a faint feeling of surprise. Usually, she would sacrifice anything to get away on their rare vacations. She had made plans very eagerly for this trip, and now she proposed to throw them overboard...!

"They'll be imprisoned," he affirmed, trying to soothe her. "They really aren't worth delaying for. This LeFevre...."

Wentworth did not see precisely what happened. He knew

that LeFevre moved so swiftly that the outlines of his body blurred. He heard Ram Singh's voice rasp out in a harsh Punjab oath and darkness smeared out the scene, or perhaps the darkness came before the curse. It was so quick…!

Wentworth hurled Nita instantly to the floor, leaped toward Ram Singh. In the darkness, men now screamed with a thin terror. One voice was choked off, gurgling, and the other ended in a gasp. From the doorway, Jackson spilled the white beam of a flashlight into the room.

Ram Singh writhed on the floor, his face purpling from a garrote which he struggled futilely to rip from his throat. His knife-sheath was empty, but the blade had not been drawn without blood. Of LeFevre's two men, only one was alive. His life was going fast through a stab wound in his chest from which Ram Singh's knife protruded. The other's head had been severed almost from his shoulders. That much Wentworth saw in a swift glance as he flung himself to Ram Singh's side and loosened the strangling silk handkerchief which had been knotted about the Sikh's throat from behind. The Hindu was still terribly weak and Jackson stood guard over both him and Nita while Wentworth raced through the penthouse in an attempt to locate LeFevre.

THE FRENCHMAN had vanished, but in the service hall, trying desperately to work the hidden lock on the door which cut off elevator and stairs, Wentworth found a girl. She wheeled at the sound of his footsteps, pressing back hard against the steel doors as if they would afford her protection. Wentworth saw that she was young and that her hair held the gleam of slumbering coals.

"I think perhaps you'd better come with me," Wentworth suggested quietly.

The girl's aspect of terror evaporated in an instant. Her body relaxed and a cynical little smile twisted her lips.

"Sure," she answered, "I think so, too." She fumbled her purse, but it was too small to hold an automatic, so Wentworth did not interfere. Her hand trembled a little as she lighted a cigarette. She struck an attitude, one hand on her hip, the other gesturing grandiloquently.

"Lay on, MacDuff," she declaimed.

Wentworth nodded. "That does it," he said. "I recognize you now. You're Margie Huron, the smart girl who jumped from a stock company into the newspaper game. There was story at the time saying you would make special investigations, using your genius for disguise…" He smiled a little. "You aren't in disguise right now, are you, Miss Huron?"

The girl answered with a saucy wrinkling of her retroussé nose. "I can see," she dropped over her shoulder, "that I'm not the hearty Elizabethan wench I think I am. I really thought, when you found me out there, that you had designs on my honor, as it is laughingly called. And, believe it or not, the idea rather frightened me."

Wentworth frowned at her swaggering back. Newspaper women always affected this hard sophistication. Sometimes it was natural, but there was still freshness about Margie Huron's eyes and the bleak thinness had not yet come to her lips. It was not strange that Wentworth should know her by name. He made a point of knowing all the newspaper men and women—the Spider made occasional skillful use of publicity....

Ram Singh was on his feet when Wentworth returned to the drawing-room and he made a single fierce stride forward, scowling so that his teeth showed white amid his bushy beard.

"Thou creature!" he cried at Margie. "'Twas thy hand put out the light and knotted that thug's weapon about my throat!"

The girl shrank back for a moment, then she shrugged and grinned impudently into Ram Singh's face. "And you stand there with your bare face hanging out—well, not so bare, is it now?— and admit that a big, strong man like you could be choked by a frail, little thing like me?"

Nita stared at her curiously. Wentworth, just behind Margie Huron, said, "I think you had better do some explaining, Miss Huron. Under those sheets are two men you helped kill!"

Jackson and Ram Singh stepped aside at Wentworth's gesture and the blood-stained sheets which covered LeFevre's two henchmen were removed. Margie's face was drained of all color and the spots of rouge on her cheeks stood out glaringly. She flicked up the brim of her felt hat with a gesture meant to be jaunty, but the trembling of her hand ruined that pose. She tucked a thumb into the armhole of her coat.

"Am I good," she boasted huskily, "or am I good?"

With a steely hand on her shoulder, Wentworth whipped her about so that she faced him. "They're electrocuting for murder these days," he said quietly.

THE FRAGILE shell of her jauntiness was badly cracked. "I didn't strangle the dusky chap," she jerked her head toward Ram Singh. "I just turned off the lights... I'd do it again, but I didn't know that..." She stared uneasily at the stained sheets.

"You couldn't be a friend of LeFevre," Wentworth said slowly. "He hasn't been here long and I don't believe you'd go for crooked money, Margie...."

She laughed brittlely. "Man, you don't know what I'd do for money! It's a rare commodity these days...."

"Therefore," Wentworth continued undisturbed, "it is obvious that you were swayed either by hatred of me, or affection for one of the prisoners."

"I'm a Communist," Margie grinned. "I hate all capitalists like you, and these poor down-trodden people...."

"Two weeks ago," Wentworth interrupted, "you were at dinner at the Cordoba Cabaret with a former stock company actor who also has found a more profitable field of work, though perhaps not quite legitimate as even his questionable acting."

Margie swayed a little on her feet. "Damn you!" she whispered. "You know...?"

"I know," Wentworth nodded, "that Ricey Charlton used to be called Charlie Hampton and was in the same cast with you, and that Ricey Charlton now runs a very profitable laundry racket, in which these two men killed here tonight worked as torpedoes. I think, Margie, that you turned out the lights so that these two men, rather than LeFevre, would escape, and that you did that because you didn't want Richard Wentworth to call on Charlton for explanations...."

Margie Huron walked up very close to Wentworth and clung to his lapels. "Charlie isn't really bad, Mr. Wentworth," she pleaded. "He isn't really. No man could be as sweet to me as Charlie is… I saw his two hoods make a try for Miss van Sloan and get taken by your Hindu. I followed in an attempt to get them loose. You see, I knew who Miss van Sloan was and who the Hindu was. Honest, I'll see that Charlie doesn't fight you anymore."

Wentworth shrugged. "That is a matter of complete indifference to me."

"I know it is," Margie cried eagerly. "I know it is, but I don't want Charlie to get hurt. Let me go and see him now. I…" Her voice broke off as the elevator door clanged open and three police men stepped out preceded by a man in plain clothes who smiled though he did not seem to be amused.

"How are you, James?" Wentworth nodded to him. "Here are the *corpora delicti.*"

Detective Jesse James took off his hat and nodded to Nita van Sloan and Jackson, the smile still on his lips, peered past Wentworth to Margie Huron.

"What's the red-headed menace doing here?" he demanded. It was plain that he and Margie knew each other. She struggled to recapture her jauntiness and managed a gamin's grin that wrinkled her nose. "It's the Indian in my ancestry, bandit. I saw Ram Singh collar a couple of men and trailed along to get their scalps." Wentworth caught the tremor in her voice, the appeal in her eyes that turned to him.

15

He laughed, "It beats all how these newspaper people are always on the scene when anything happens."

Jesse James grunted, muttered something about a turned-up nose for news, and went to work.

WHEN POLICE had gone, Margie Huron threw her arms around Wentworth's neck and implanted an emphatic kiss on the point of his chin, which was the highest point she could reach. "You're a honey," she said swiftly, "Ricey Charlton won't bother you any more..." She whirled saucily to Nita. "Excuse it, please, but he *is* nice, you know." She swaggered out the door. Nita laughed, thrust her arm through Wentworth's. "She's rather a dear, Dick."

Wentworth persuaded Nita to go out to dinner and the theater as they had planned, and throughout the evening, he tried to extract a promise from her to sail on the *Normandie* and continue the vacation in the Tyrol. Nita's lips grew firm in refusal. She was still angry....

"I won't sail," she said stubbornly, "until that insulting Frenchman is laid by the heels. It isn't like you to run from a fight...." She regretted that thrust instantly. "Oh, I know it isn't that, Dick, and I know you want us to have that trip to the Tyrol."

Wentworth tightened an arm about her shoulders. "I do believe, Nita, that the fighting virus has got into your veins at last!"

She shook her head and her chestnut curls were tumbled into disorder with her violence. Then she laughed. "Maybe, Dick. But I mean it. I won't go until LeFevre is in prison. I guess it sounds funny, but oh, Dick, it's damnable to always have our happiest moments interrupted by these slimy little crooks, and I won't have it! We're going to teach them a lesson with LeFevre that they won't ever forget!"

Wentworth shrugged. He was still inclined to be amused at the whole thing. LeFevre had fumbled so badly on all sides... It was true that his vicious killing of his two men betokened a man who would be well served, through fear if by no other means. Still, Wentworth could not take him seriously. LeFevre was out of his depth in American crime circles, with American police methods. Even without the Spider's help, the police and Federal men would snare LeFevre....

Wentworth toyed idly with his keys while the private elevator lofted them toward the fifteenth floor where his duplex penthouse was situated. "We've still got an hour before sailing," he said slowly. "We're both fully packed... perhaps, I can persuade you?"

Nita shook her head, her full, soft lips compressed. "You can persuade me by putting LeFevre behind the bars!"

Wentworth laughed, handed Nita from the elevator and stood rigidly staring. In the middle of the door to his apartment was a neat, white card, such as men of society use. Wentworth reached it in a bound and read there only one thing, the name of Jules LeFevre, handsomely engraved. He slapped open the door, a gun flying to his hand from its under-arm holster and a great cry sprang to his throat. The apartment was a wreck. He missed at once an exquisite Corot which had hung in the hall. The floors were bare of the rich Aubussons he had traveled the world to collect.

RICHARD WENTWORTH

He leaped across the hall to the doorway of the drawing-room and saw that here, too, the looting had been carried out with the perfection and thoroughness of a man who knew the full value of the things he took. The oath that pushed out between Wentworth's teeth was not for this. It was for the pitiful spectacle that met his eyes at the room's further end. Hanging by their hands from nails that pierced their palms, his three servants sagged unconscious across the archway of the terrace doors. They had been flogged until the flesh hung in bloody ribbons from their backs!

CHAPTER 2
DAWN OF MADNESS

WENTWORTH SAID to Nita not to enter the room, but to call a doctor at once. Then he rushed to the assistance of his men. Ram Singh lifted a heavy head and his bearded lips in a transient smile.

"*Wah, sahib,*" he whispered, "thy servants are not men, but

19

mice! The old one first, Master. Thy servant shall be last for that it was he who brought this… disaster."

Wentworth snatched chairs and set them beneath the feet of Jackson and Ram Singh, lifted the body of old Jenkyns, the butler who had served his father before him, down into his arms. Nita came to his side with a hammer and a pair of pincers she had snatched from the butler's pantry. Her voice was strained, but calm.

"You hold him up," she said steadily, "I'll… pull the nails."

Wentworth's eyes shot to her with gratitude. She stood upon a chair and eased the nails from the wood beam into which they had been driven, pulled them out of the lacerated flesh. Jackson still sagged unconscious from the nails and, though Ram Singh protested violently, he was the next to be freed. When one hand was freed, he took the hammer from Nita and carelessly wrenched out the second spike himself. He stepped down from the chair which Wentworth had placed—and collapsed in a heap on the floor.…

Not until the doctor had labored over the terribly beaten men for nearly an hour was it possible for Wentworth to get the story of what had happened. LeFevre had hidden in the dumbwaiter shaft and had struck down each of them separately: knocking out Jenkyns, catching Ram Singh from behind when the noise of Jenkyns' fall brought him at a dead run, lying in wait for Jackson, who had gone out on an errand for Jenkyns. Afterward LeFevre's men had come and assisted in the fiendish torture.

"Two weeks at least before the strongest of them can leave his bed," the doctor told Wentworth briefly. "They'll be better off in a hospital. I'm afraid that Jenkyns…" He saw the stolidity that bit Wentworth's pain at mention of the silver-haired old butler. "Shock, you know. His heart is… old."

When the three men, drugged almost to unconsciousness, had been carried to a private hospital, Wentworth walked heavily to the drawing-room where Nita had long since withdrawn. She had discarded her exquisite evening clothing for a tailored, dark suit. She smiled, but her lips were tight.

"You and I are in this together," she said. "I don't intend to be sent away for protection."

Wentworth's head lifted and he bent tenderly over her chair. "What would I do without you, darling?"

"Fight," she told him briefly, then she lifted her face for his kiss. It was like her that she did not taunt him with his earlier determination to go abroad despite LeFevre's challenge. "What do you want me to do?"

"First of all," he said quietly, "we'll call on Kirkpatrick at police headquarters and see what he's doing. Then I'll want you to find and keep an eye on Margie Huron…."

Nita started. "I wondered why you let her go."

Wentworth nodded. "Charlton has been in hiding since that killing in the laundry racket two days ago. She'll lead us to him, I hope. I'm taking another trail. Do nothing without letting me know. I'm going to need you, Nita."

WHEN WENTWORTH had changed to the dark, handsomely tailored tweeds he favored, they drove in his Hispano-Suiza roadster to police headquarters. It was there Wentworth was sure to find his friend, Stanley Kirkpatrick, who had been

21

New York's police commissioner through a half-dozen changing political regimes. To Kirkpatrick, as to Wentworth, the suppression of crime was not a business, but a high vocation. The commissioner would be on the job, certainly, after such a happening as the torture in Wentworth's apartment.

Kirkpatrick saw them immediately, rising and striding to meet Wentworth and Nita with outstretched hands, his long, saturnine face even more grave than usual.

"This is terrible, Dick," he cried. "We're doing all we can, but the truth of the matter is that somebody slipped up badly. We didn't even know that LeFevre was in the country!"

Wentworth nodded. "You'll know, Kirk, that if I mention protection, it's not a criticism of you or the department. I am convinced that LeFevre has powerful patrons in the city, perhaps among the police themselves! Otherwise, he would not have dared to begin matters with such a high hand. Furthermore, he could not have formed an alliance with Ricey Charlton so quickly. He's been brought here for some purpose, Kirk—some dire purpose. I don't mean my personal destruction. LeFevre did not behave as though that were a matter of great importance." He smiled slightly, and strangely it made his face only more grim. "He did not even seem much impressed with my abilities."

Kirkpatrick stood very erectly always, but tonight be seemed bracing himself against an attack. He parted his spiked mustache with thumb and forefingers. "Have you any suggestion...?"

He slapped fist to palm. "By George, Dick, it comes to me! Today, three men communicated with me about threats they had received. All of the men are very wealthy, in the millionaire class, in fact, and accustomed to receiving threats. They guard constantly against attack, but these threats were different…" He strode, long-legged, to his desk, pressed a buzzer and spoke into an enunciator on his desk.

"The Lyman file," he ordered crisply. He strode back to Wentworth, movements jerky with aroused energy. "They were extortion notes up to a certain point, and that was the threat of violence. Dick, these letters uniformly threatened to drive *the man or some member of his family insane…!*

Kirkpatrick caught the file from the secretary who brought them in. The man bowed respectfully to Wentworth before he left. They knew him at police headquarters and they respected him for far more than the friendship they knew was his and Kirkpatrick's… Kirkpatrick snatched out a letter. "Look…."

Wentworth held the note gingerly between fingerprints that he pressed to its edges. "You are summoned to attend on the night of May 19 in the Board of Trade offices," it read, "a meeting of the Board of Directors of Insanity, Inc. There is a slight difference between this and other director meetings to which you are accustomed. Instead of being paid, you will pay for the privilege. The fee is one hundred thousand dollars, and it must be in cash. This will purchase you a single share of Insanity, Inc. and the possession of that share will protect you and your family from insanity. Should you make the mistake of not attending this meeting, your son, Horace, will go mad at precisely twenty-five minutes after eight—twenty-five minutes after you are due at the meeting—and the results of this madness you will not fancy."

THE MESSAGE was unsigned and, aside from the fact that it was typed on a very excellent quality vellum paper, there was nothing to identify it.

"No fingerprints?" Wentworth asked.

Kirkpatrick shook his head "That's the queer part of it. All

The Spider's bullet bored
through the killer's skull!

24

of these notes were signed with a fingerprint, the fingerprint of Colonel Delancey Hanson!"

Wentworth started. Hanson was the police expert on fingerprints, one of the world's greatest. It would be almost impossible for his fingerprints to be taken without his knowledge, yet it was unthinkable that he should be connected with the extortion notes. "May I ask what plans you are making?" Wentworth asked slowly.

Kirkpatrick made a choppy gesture with his hand. "Guards, of course. The Board of Trade directors' room actually has been engaged by someone tomorrow night. The man who made the arrangements answers the description of LeFevre as nearly as I can obtain it from the Board of Trade secretary. I didn't realize that until you brought up the theory of some major project." His lips twisted in a queer smile. "In fact, from what they said, I thought that some hoax was being played, for the descriptions tallied very closely with my own!"

Wentworth met his fiend's queer smile. "Superficially, you and LeFevre are somewhat alike...." He pivoted as a jangling bell note came from the police teletype printer in the corner of the room. Nita was nearest the instrument, which connected not only with all precincts and state police headquarters, but also, at will, with New Jersey and Pennsylvania systems. Nita uttered a low cry....

"The Lyman home!" she called. "A report that a crazy man has killed several people!"

Wentworth and Kirkpatrick stood rigidly, staring at each other through a long moment, then they dashed for the machine and stood watching while the rhythmic clatter pounded out letters which slowly became words… Kirkpatrick raced back to his phone, called the Lyman home directly and, after a long ringing, the connection went through.

"Sullivan? Good! I'm glad you're there! This is Kirkpatrick. What happened?" While Kirkpatrick listened to the man whose voice made rasping noises in the instrument, his face grew first grave, and then savage. There was a harsh rage in the lines of his mouth. Finally, the voice stopped, and Kirkpatrick spoke: "Hold every person in that house! Sequester all food supplies and drinking fluids! Put them under lock and key. Yes, I'll be right out."

His eyes swung almost absently to Wentworth. He seemed dazed by the things he had heard. "Lyman's son, Horace, went mad suddenly in the night. He killed his sister and mother before his father shot him down. Horace is sane again but likely to lose his mind from grief. Lyman is prostrated."

Wentworth felt cold trembling pass over his body. LeFevre had struck more swiftly than he could possibly have feared! Wentworth had no doubt that it was LeFevre and he cursed himself bitterly for his failure to recognize the peril in the man and destroy him while he had him at his mercy.

"But the note said tomorrow night!" Wentworth muttered hoarsely.

Kirkpatrick nodded jerkily. He had got to his feet and was holstering a long barreled revolver he took from his desk drawer. It was characteristic of him that despite his frantic haste, he paused to take a gardenia from a desk vase for his buttonhole. "Yes, there was a note stating that it was done as an object lesson because Lyman had communicated with police. Yet we kept the extortion note an absolute secret! Not three men besides myself knew of it. The note was signed the same way, with Hanson's thumb print..." He stiffened, staring into Wentworth's face. "It's unthinkable," he whispered. "Absolutely unthinkable, but *Colonel Hanson was one of the three men who knew!*"

It was not necessary that Wentworth urge Kirkpatrick to start at once an inquiry into Colonel Hanson's affairs and history. Before this, men in positions of public trust had been known to consort and plot with criminals. Hurried guards were also thrown about the other two men to lodge complaints with police, but so far the madness which LeFevre had loosed on Lyman had not struck them....

IT WAS late when finally Nita and Wentworth returned to his apartment and both were weary when they separated at the door of her suite. Nita clung to him....

"I'm a little bit afraid, Dick," she said slowly. "Insanity is a terrible weapon in criminal hands."

Wentworth nodded. "I had intended to change to a hotel rather than attempt to find trustworthy servants. I think we'll still leave out the servants, but it would be wise to stay here. And eat nothing that has not been prepared by our own hands! This insanity is almost certainly the result of some drugs..." He forced himself to laugh. "You have never had occasion to taste my cooking, dear. Perhaps it'll be a surprise."

Nita grimaced. "I hope the surprise is pleasant!"

Wentworth and Nita both worked the following day in an attempt to locate Ricey Charlton, but Charlton's friends refused information to Wentworth. Margie Huron, whom Nita followed, tended strictly to her newspaper work. However, as the time approached when the Board of Directors of Insanity, Inc. was to meet, Wentworth hurried back to his penthouse. He had refused Kirkpatrick's invitation to attend the meeting with the police watch. He knew that Kirkpatrick would make the best possible arrangement to snare LeFevre should he or his accomplices attempt to collect the money the threatened men had been instructed to bring. There was no doubt that there would be many more than the three who had appealed to police. Lyman, naturally, would not attend and was under heavy guard at his home, but there was little hope that any others would have the courage to remain away after the terrible tragedy at the Lyman home. They would be thoroughly terrified. Wentworth also made his plans to attend, but not in his own personality.

At his home, he sped to his vaulted music room and, before the pipe organ which filled the entire end, he tapped rhythmically on the orifices of three pipes. Faint ghosts of music sounded as the columns of air vibrated. He stopped abruptly, and strode rapidly along the paneled wall. One of the sections receded a few inches and slid noiselessly aside. He stepped through the secret doorway into a compact dressing-room whose walls held racks of clothing. There was a table whose mirror was ringed with

29

brilliant neon lights and a rack of a hundred make up materials with which Wentworth was brilliantly deft. He went skillfully to work upon his face....

Under the expert manipulation of his fingers, an ointment tautened his cheeks until the skin stretched tightly over the bones, became sallow and harsh. His lips vanished and the mouth became a lipless gash, the nose a thin, predatory beak. That was all, except for shaggy brows and a black wig whose lank hair fell almost to his shoulders.

The face that stared back at Richard Wentworth now was no longer his own keenly handsome countenance. It was sinister and darkly ominous, the slitted eyes held a coldness that was like the coldness of death. Quickly, he arose to his feet, drew a black, slouch hat low on his brows and swung a long, black cape about his shoulders. His lithe figure disappeared and across the tiny dressing-room limped a hunch-back of furtive, ominous mien.

If any man had seen him now, and that man were in his heart guilty of crime, he would have fled with screams of absolute terror. For now, Richard Wentworth was the Spider! And the Spider brought swift and ruthless judgment to those who sinned against their fellow men!

ON THE far side of the dressing-room, he manipulated a lever and peered through a slot into the service hallway and stairs of his apartment. He nodded with satisfaction, touched another button and stepped through the doorway which opened. The service elevator moved downward without sound, and through the half-dark of the cellar, Wentworth made his unmolested way. He had purchased the entire building so that he could control its tenancy and personnel and the superintendent never watched very closely the strange figures who came and went by this furtive, hidden way. He thought that his employer did secret police business in which he used many spies. He thought that these furtive men were those spies. How could he know that they were really only one man, in any one of the myriad identities he chose to assume?

In a nearby private garage upon an alley, Wentworth kept a small car whose powerful motor he had personally designed. It was not a pretentious seeming vehicle, but its stream lining was perfect and a supercharger boosted its motor above a hundred-seventy five horsepower. It was completely bullet-proof. Through the crowded streets of early evening, the Spider drove inconspicuously until he was within a block of the Gaillard Building, in which the Board of Trade had offices. For the few moments that he walked openly along the street, Wentworth threw off his limping, hunch-backed pace. The black hat sat jauntily on his head and the cape was tossed back over his shoulders. He became merely a gentleman with a slight eccentricity of dress—if the passerby did not glimpse his face. The watchman in an office building not too far from the Gaillard did not see his face until he had unfastened the doors. Then he reeled back, snatching for his revolver. Wentworth's hand flicked out with the speed of light and compressed certain nerves in the throat which dropped the man, instantly unconscious, to the floor. He locked the doors again, placed the man in his chair so that he seemed asleep, and ran the elevator to the top floor. The man would be unconscious for a half-hour and by that time, the Spider would be gone…!

It was simple to make his way across roofs to the Gaillard Building. He tossed a light, silken rope to a window and lassoed a hook intended for a window-washer's belt. His superb muscles drew him lightly up the rope. The window yielded instantly to a slender lever of chrome steel and he was inside. The Board of Trade offices were three stories above him; stairs and elevators probably would be watched. He elected to continue his upward progress by means of the windows and the fine silken rope scarcely as large in diameter as a lead pencil, nevertheless had a tensile strength of seven hundred pounds! The police were familiar enough with that powerful cordage. They called it the Spider's *web!*

Wentworth ascended to the floor above the lighted windows of the Board of Trade offices, looped his line over the hooks as before and seated himself in a sling to wait. By swaying a few inches to one side, he could gaze into either of two windows of the Board of Trade Directors' room. No one was present, but in the center of the table reposed a gray cloth bag such as mail is shipped in, and beside it lay a piece of stationery on which typing appeared. Wentworth eyed it with tightening lips. LeFevre, if the extortionist were really he, had already been in the room and left instructions for his victims!

With his usual rare good judgment, Kirkpatrick had left the message undisturbed, nor were his guards in evidence. They would have the building sealed tightly against ordinary ingress, but there was no reason why some of LeFevre's *Apaches*—

beyond a doubt he had brought some of his more able hench-men with him for his invasion of America—could not climb to the window as Wentworth had. The burglars of Paris were clever and were used to climbing among the chimney pots....

THAT MIGHT be their mode of escape, but Wentworth thought that instead of picking a way into the building after the guards were placed, LeFevre would have his men in the build-ing since before the offices had emptied. In that way, he would eliminate fifty percent of the risk.

It was five minutes before eight when the first of LeFevre's victims entered the meeting-room. He gripped the briefcase in which apparently he carried his money as vehemently as if it were a weapon, his jaw jutted. Men who had carved a fortune amid vicious competition did not surrender easily to criminal mulcters. Wentworth knew him, of course. Harrison Fishman, as famous for his Eastern explorations as for his two-fisted treatment of Wall Street. He read the note on the desk and his hard-chiseled lips moved in what were plainly curses. He emptied the contents of his briefcase into the mail-sack on the long table and took a seat, began chewing on an unlighted cigar.

After him, other men entered rapidly and, in amazement, Wentworth identified them. Leading industrialists, men with millions of capital at work for them, a banker of international reputation, a politician of ill repute, but high financial rating. One after another, they dumped thick wads of bills into the mail-sack on the table and threw themselves angrily into chairs. They eyed each other cautiously, or talked in half-furtive whis-pers; the air rapidly became thick with tobacco smoke. And still nothing happened. The tenseness of the men was communicated to Wentworth. He threw searching glances into the darkness below and above him, but could detect no movement. His view was somewhat hampered by the awnings at the windows…. The distance-softened sounds of the night drifted up to him, the muted roar of the traffic, and it seemed incredible that on this placid May night, madness and death should stalk through the city streets. It was a time of year when humanity's thoughts grew gentle….

The panel of the wall swung outward without any warning at all and Wentworth saw that it concealed a large safe whose door swung open at the same time. From within the vault, a dapper man, holding a gun in each hand, stepped out.

The waiting men sprang to their feet. Harrison Fishman took angry strides forward, his jaw set solidly, his fists knotted at his sides. He was a splendid figure of a man and his defiant outburst, deep-throated and harsh, came to Wentworth where he waited outside the window, peering about its edge.

"You can't get away with this," Fishman declared, "I have paid my fee because of the dastardly attack made on Lyman's family, but I shall seek satisfaction!"

Wentworth's lips twitched in a grim smile. How many times had beleaguered humanity cried out to its despoilers in those words, "You can't get away with it!" But criminals did. In the end, they'd pay, but meantime, humanity suffered and men and women died. A tiny point of fury burned in Wentworth's skull. This man with the guns was one of those who had caused Lyman's son to ruin his life with insane murders of those he loved most! This was one of those who had flogged the Spider's servants into the hospital. A gun slid into Wentworth's palm, but one of the men within was before him.

A GUN crashed and the dapper man spun crazily about on one foot, the other leg whirling limply wide as he fought for balance against the impact of lead. His shoulders struck the steel door of the safe and he braced there. Though his whole body flinched with the sledge hammer blow of a second bullet, he still did not fall. His two guns began to speak as Fishman went down, threshing, and another man pitched across the table, beating it with impotent fists before Wentworth's gun smashed through glass and his bullet bored the killer's skull. The two-gun bandit seemed crucified to the steel door by the Spider's lead, incapable even of falling, and he stayed that way through throbbing seconds while men in uniform poured into the room from two side doors. Kirkpatrick was in their lead, long-barreled thirty-eight in his right hand. His eyes shot swiftly over the room and his sharp orders sent men to succor the gunman's two victims. Wentworth remained hidden outside the window. He did not think that the broken window would attract any special attention. A wild bullet from within might have caused it... and he did not believe the attack was over. LeFevre was too shrewd to play his full hand at once....

Wentworth was aware abruptly that two of the wealthy victims were paying no heed to the police or to their companions. One circled the room in a queer uncertain way. The other stood staring down at Harrison Fishman, who was sitting on the floor, gripping a wounded leg. A cold touch of dread made

Wentworth shiver. Those men…! They were the two who had defied the demand for money and informed police. Lyman had paid by having his son go mad. Was it possible that these two…? Kirkpatrick must be warned. Wentworth got his feet to the window sill and in that instant, madness struck terribly.

One of the men caught up a heavy chair and brained Fishman. The other snatched a gun from a policeman and opened point-blank fire upon the other men in the room, shooting both at his previous companions and at the police. Wentworth saw an officer take a bullet through the face that tore off the top of his head, saw a financier reel backward in horror and crumple with hot lead in his belly, and, above him, Wentworth was aware of movement, of a tremor in the silken rope that alone held him from a plunge of more than fifty feet to the roof of the building below.

Quick as light, his gun jerked upward, his eyes questing. He hesitated for a moment, knowing that a shot would betray him instantly to the police inside. Embroiled in a life-and-death struggle, they would fire immediately on what seemed to them a new menace. Even if they recognized him, it would not deter them.

Rather, it would make their efforts to kill him more frenzied. For to the police, the Spider was a hunted criminal, a man sought for a hundred kills. It did not matter to them that those he killed always richly deserved death, that they were those who must otherwise evade justice. There was a standing reward of fifty thousand dollars on his head…!

These thoughts were lightning flashes in his brain, and his

hesitation was not a second in duration. He was aware of a dark figure in the window above, caught the gleam of a knife edged against the strands of the silken rope. He must take the chance of a shot from within. He jerked his gun upward and the blast of the shot deafened him. The recoil of his shot hurled him into space, or so it seemed. He knew that his lead had sped true, but it had been instants too late. The knife had cut the silk! Backward, head first, the Spider plunged toward the death that awaited him five stories below!

CHAPTER 3
GUNS OF DOOM

R ATIONAL THOUGHT in a moment of utter disaster is not the gift of many men, but Wentworth's brain had been trained through necessity in literally hundreds of deadly encounters. Even in the moment when he felt the rope sag limply in his hands, he did the only thing which might save him from death. It was futile to grasp at the window sill, but he did not thrust strongly with his legs as most men instinctively would have done. Instead, he dropped as close to the side of the building as possible. He had one hope: the awnings. If he could manage to hook arms or legs into one of them… A grip with the hands would not suffice, for it would inevitably be snatched loose by the momentum of his fall.

Wentworth was still half-dazed with the horror of the thing that was happening up there in the directors' room. Two madmen whom police would frantically try not to injure were slaughtering their friends. LeFevre need only extinguish the lights, drop down from the floor above where his men had cut the Spider's *web* and snatch the bag of money. Escape would be simple....

The first awning shot upward past Wentworth while his head still pointed downward, his back to the wall, and two more had passed him futilely before he succeeded in somersaulting to an upright position. His spread arms created a sail of his cape which served to steady him in that position. Two more awnings were below him. He was risking every chance of survival on the chance of snatching one. If he struck in this position, his legs would be crumpled, the bones driven like bayonets into his body. He clawed out frantically with arms and legs for the awning, managed to grab it—with his fingers, no more. There was a violent wrench, a rip and tear of cloth and the singing snap of steel, Wentworth's desperate hold was torn loose with a jerk that seemed to unhinge his shoulders and left his arms numb and useless. He plunged on, but that grab at life had accomplished one thing. It had slowed his speed and it had swung him a little closer to the building.

Dazed, wracked with the pain in his arm, he still managed to try with his legs for the awning just below him. It was the last one. If he missed... He was aware of a dark body tumbling, tumbling down close above him, the man he had shot in the instant of severing the ropes. They had been only a story apart, and though they fell at the same speed, the awning had checked Wentworth a little. The light was out in the directors' room.

Those things the Spider saw as his legs reached for the awning. It was folded up, the cloth making a hammock against the stone of the building's wall. Strong cloth, but it would break like tissue paper, and....

His feet plunged into the hammock of cloth, smashed through. The steel frame raked his calves, was ripped from it, fastenings on one side, caught under Wentworth's arms. Something brushed his shoulders, struck with a wet crunch as the final mooring of the awning gave way and dropped Wentworth the last few feet to the roof below.

He struck with stunning force, but he was conscious of a huge elation. The two awnings had broken his fall tremendously and the body of the man he had shot in the act of murder had fallen beneath him to cushion his fall. The breath was driven from his body. For long seconds, he lay motionless, then he reeled to his feet with a prayer of thanksgiving in his heart. Now that the thing was over, he felt a quivering in every fiber of his being. Never, he realized, had the Spider been nearer to death, nor more helpless to avert his doom....

He stared up at the window from which he had fallen, his arms torn with pain, his nerves jangling. Shots still crashed, men screamed, but no figure bulked against the sky. If LeFevre had planned to use this route, apparently the death of his assistant had turned him aside. Wentworth knew that even if LeFevre walked directly into his arms, he would be helpless to avert his escape. He could not even grip a gun....

HIS BRAIN worked in queer, broken flashes. As if to confirm his helplessness, he fumbled inside his coat for his second gun—and could scarcely tell when he touched the butt. His other gun had fallen. He got on his knees and looked for it, dimly irritated at the presence of this crushed, dead thing which might hide the weapon he sought and which he could not move.

Overhead, a gun blasted more loudly and he stared upward to see powder flame lancing toward him. The body beside him jerked to the impact of lead. Wentworth staggered to his feet, fled on erratic feet, which almost spilled him a half dozen times, toward the roof scuttle by which he had ascended. The gun kept stuttering and bullets whined past, but he made the scuttle safely and tumbled down into the building. The elevator was whining like a dog which has lost the trail. Men coming up, police coming up to trap him! His feet stumbled as he plodded toward the steps, his brain seemed numb....

"Escape!" he whispered to himself. "I must escape…!"

He had descended two floors before his brain seemed to clear a little. He looked about him desperately. A door at his left hand read: *Harry Finch, Advertising.*

An idea stung him with its clarity. He fumbled a thin, hooked probe of surgical steel from a belt of narrow pockets about his waist and managed finally, with numbed fingers to pick the lock. He shot the latch, hurried across the inner office and switched on lights. Swiftly, he threw his cape into a file cabinet drawer, tossed hat and coat upon a rack, ripped an envelope at random from the case and scattered its contents over the desk top. He

slumped into the chair, got a pen
from the drawer and began to read
swiftly.

"*If Beans Could Talk*—" a head-
line shouted at him. In smaller
type: "They would say, 'We prefer to be canned by Halliman.
Their sauce is our bosom friend.'"

Laughter pushed at Wentworth's lips and for a moment he
gave way to it wildly. He choked it down, knowing it for the
reaction of that perilous drop and the severe shake-up he had
experienced. His stomach rebelled, his heart pounded with a
heavy sickness. He staggered to the window, retching....

Presently, he felt a return to normalcy, though the pain of his
wrenched shoulders still stabbed him fiercely. He rumpled his
hair, shoved a pencil behind his ear and dragged on an eye-shade.
Then he went out of the office, leaving the door open, and rang
the elevator bell. He could hear it pealing, funereally through
the empty corridors and presently the cage came to a halt at
his floor. The door whipped open and a policeman thrust out a
belligerent chin.

"What the hell?" he demanded.

Wentworth staggered back, his face twisted in exaggerated
surprise. Then he grinned. "What the hell, yourself?" he said.
"How the hell do you expect a guy to get his work done if you
keep on shooting? Who's killed?"

The policeman glared at him, became elaborately polite. "So
sorry our shooting bothered you. We won't let it happen again.

Sa-ay, 'bo, the Spider's loose in this building. If you're wise, you'll get out damned fast. He eats little boys like you!"

Wentworth let his eyes open incredulously, his mouth sag. He acted out superbly a man trying not to show fear. "I'm just about through anyway," he gulped. "Say, how about you taking me down to the first floor, and letting me out?"

The cop hesitated and Wentworth groped in his pocket and found a ten dollar bill. "I'll be right back!" he called.

TWO MINUTES later, the grinning cop ushered him out of the front door of the building and Wentworth hurried along the street, casting many backward glances. At the corner, he turned and sprinted. Within less than a minute, he was at the doors of the Gaillard Building. The last of the make-up had been stripped from his face now, and the policeman on guard at the outer door saluted him respectfully.

"Let no one out of here at all," Wentworth told him, "and that includes your fellow officers. Understand? I'll get confirmation from Commissioner Kirkpatrick at once."

The man hesitated. Wentworth pushed past him impatiently, went to the telephone at the information desk and called the Board of Trade Offices. Kirkpatrick came to the phone quickly and Wentworth repeated his request.

"If you'll give that order, Kirk, I'll come up and tell you why," he said briefly. "Otherwise, I wish you'd come down here. I won't leave the door until…" He whirled away from the instrument, challenged a uniformed man headed toward the doors. "Stay in the building," he said curtly, "Commissioner's orders!"

Over the phone, Kirkpatrick was saying, "All right. Give me Sergeant Heinz. He's there in the foyer somewhere."

The uniformed man he had challenged glowered at him. "Who are you that you're giving orders?"

"Sergeant Heinz!" Wentworth raised his voice. "Sergeant Heinz! Commissioner wants you on the phone!"

He met the officer's glare firmly. "Commissioner's orders are that no one leaves the building, including officers."

The man laughed. "I should listen to you!"

He started toward the door. Wentworth reached his side in two long strides and whipped the man around. It gave his shoulder a stab of pain, but his face showed nothing of that.

"You won't leave the building," he insisted flatly. Suspicion made his blood race. With a quick movement, he reached out his hand and tapped the policeman's abdomen with the flat of his hand. The man cursed, reached for his gun and Wentworth laughed out loud and struck twice with a surge and snap of his body that put all his weight into the blows. The man reeled back against the wall and slumped to the floor. The door guard leaped forward, drawing his revolver, but Wentworth ignored him, crouched over the uniformed man on the floor and ripped open his coat. A handful of thousand dollars bills fluttered into sight. The door guard gasped.

"This is one of the extortionists in disguise!" Wentworth said sharply. "Don't let anyone else leave the building!"

Moments later, Kirkpatrick barged out of the elevator. His quick glance took in the scene and its meaning instantly. His crisp accents rose; his orders flew swiftly. Not only was no man to be allowed to leave the building, but fresh squads were to be called out from headquarters. And every man in the building was to be searched. Kirkpatrick glowered down the unconscious man in police clothes.

"Not an impostor," he said, "The man is actually a cop, a disgrace to his uniform. Looks like you were right about corruption in the department, Dick…" He shook his long, angular head. "I'll wipe it out. I'll rip it out by the roots…."

The scowl lingered on his face, but as he met Wentworth's eyes, his lips stirred in a slight smile. "By the way, Dick, your friend, the Spider was on the scene tonight. Apparently, he took a bad spill on the roof of the building next door. We found his web and it had been cut with a knife. He killed the man who did that, of course…" His eyes were quizzical. He had no doubt of his friend's identity as the Spider, and had told him as much, though Wentworth never admitted it. Kirkpatrick was rigorous in the performance of his duties. He had warned his friend that if the proof of his operations as the Spider ever fell into his hands, he would prosecute him to the last atom of his power, but that until that time, he and Wentworth would continue as friends. The truth of the matter was that Kirkpatrick intensely admired the work of the Spider, only condemned the fact that the sinister hunchback operated outside the law and was himself judge and jury and executioner. All of this was in his glance. "Quite a fall, it must have been," he murmured "Did you know, Dick, that the back of your left trouser leg has a bad tear in it? And that there is gravel such as is on the roof next door in your right trouser cuff? Couldn't be proved, of course, but…."

Wentworth smiled faintly, "To hell with your innuendos, Kirk. What are you talking about?"

"The weather," Kirkpatrick told him mildly. "Shall I tell you what happened upstairs, or do you already know?"

WENTWORTH WAS aware of the effort that his lightness cost Kirkpatrick. There were drawn, harsh lines about his mouth and a tiredness about his eyes that bespoke of fatigue. Kirkpatrick was never a man to give way to despair or to any emotion. The extent of their warm friendship would be expressed in a handclasp, no more. He began to talk without waiting for an answer. The two men who had gone mad had succeeded in killing a policeman and three of their associates before they had been subdued. In the midst of the battle, the lights had gone out. Kirkpatrick had attempted to reach the bag of money, but had been struck over the head. When he got to his feet again, the money was gone. Someone had shouted that the Spider had the money and there had been some shooting from the window....

"Any suggestions, Dick, about tracking down LeFevre?"

Wentworth shook his head slowly, "Only one. Find Charlton or some of his men." He felt an immense heaviness. They had scored on LeFevre, but the mystery had only deepened. It was clear that someone high in authority in the city was his ally, perhaps his superior in the perilous game that was being played with death and wealth and souls....

The search of the police, completed, showed no other trace of the stolen money and it became apparent that Wentworth's intercession had been a little too late. The guard at the door recalled that a half dozen officers had gone out, but he could remember only one of them by name. That one, when located, was on his way back to the building and had a legitimate excuse for absence.

"I have still another suggestion," Kirkpatrick said grimly. "I am going to take this officer we caught to the Police Academy."

Wentworth glanced at him quickly. He knew well enough what Kirkpatrick meant by that. In the police academy was a sound-proofed pistol range. No matter what outcry the prisoner made there, he could not be heard outside. Kirkpatrick's jaw was grim. He was no proponent of brutal methods, but his anger had been thoroughly aroused. The Police Department was his entire life and it hurt him with the pain of a personal injury that one of its members should throw in with criminals. Wentworth knew a cold fury himself. There were times when the third degree was justified, and he felt that this was one. He went with Kirkpatrick to his limousine, Sergeant Heinz thrusting the handcuffed prisoner ahead. Kirkpatrick took the wheel himself and sent the car through the streets with vicious speed, the siren kicking a path through the traffic. He maintained a rigid silence. No one spoke to the prisoner, whose name was Strauss. Heinz's glare could not be mistaken. He felt that the disgrace of a country-man touched him also and Wentworth knew there would be no mercy from him.

Kirkpatrick unlocked the Academy Building and Strauss, seeing him lead the way toward the basement stairs, shrank back. He made no sound, even when Heinz punched him heavily on the nape, but it was plain that he was terribly frightened. He had to be almost dragged down the steps and through the sound-proofed doors of the pistol range. Heinz whirled him around then and slammed a beefy fist full into his face so that Strauss, whimpering, protesting hoarsely, slammed against the wall. Heinz nailed him there with another punch to the face and Strauss slipped to the floor.

"That will do, Sergeant," Kirkpatrick said, his voice rasping. "You can't have all the pleasure yourself." He gripped Strauss by the collar of his tunic, jerked him to his feet. With steely fingers, he ripped off the man's badge, then threw it into his face.

"Don't talk," he said fiercely. "Don't open your mouth."
HE LAID his knuckles against the man's cheek and twisted his fist slowly. It didn't hurt much, but it was threatening.

"I don't want you to talk," he said softly. "It would rob me of my chance. I don't like crooks, Strauss, and I don't like crooked policemen. And you're both. Don't open your mouth...."

Strauss fell on his knees and pleaded. "For God's sake, Commissioner, don't rough me up. I'll talk. I'll tell you everything I know. That French guy said everything was all right. He said he could fix things swell for me, no matter what happened."

Kirkpatrick said gently, "I see. And how was this to be done?"

Wentworth watched him with a sense of amazement. He had known, of course, that Kirkpatrick could be flinty hard where his duty was concerned, but this was a new facet of his character. To be sure, he had operated chiefly by threat so far, but Wentworth knew that he would use force, too, if necessary.

Strauss blubbered as Sergeant Heinz slapped him across the nape with the barrel of his revolver. "Don't hit me again. Please don't hit me again! I'll talk. I'll tell everything! The Frenchman said Colonel Hanson was in on it, and…."

The crack of the pistol was strangely flat in the sound-proofed room. Strauss' body lunged backward on the calves of his kneeling legs, then his feet popped out and thumped to the floor. They made little spasmodic kickings as the last flicker of his life went out of him. Kirkpatrick flung himself face down on the floor and rolled, snatching for his revolver. Wentworth had not bothered to fall. He dodged aside, pivoting on his heel and as he faced about his gun was in his hand, but he held his fire. There was no one to shoot at. The double swing doors at the entrance swayed a little, but there was no other movement and no sound at all.

The tableau could not have held for half a second, then Wentworth bounded across the room, punched open the doors and went through gun first. The hallway outside was empty, the two other doors that opened off it were locked. While he tested them, Kirkpatrick had sprung past him up the stairs and Wentworth followed, rounded a platform and saw that the Commissioner was standing motionless on next to the top step. His voice came down, acidly.

"Nice work, Detective James."

He hurried to Kirkpatrick's side and peered along the dim main hall. Toward him moved two figures, one whose compact wide shoulders identified him instantly as Detective Jesse James, the other was a woman.

"Why not use the handcuffs, Mr. Jesse Bandit James?" she jeered. "It would be so much more business-like and it might save you from a charge of unnecessary favoritism."

Wentworth recognized the voice with a vertical creasing of his brows. Margie Huron! He shook his head vehemently. The pieces of the puzzle did not fit together. Surely, she would not have shot down a man… He recalled sharply that, whether intentionally or not, she had helped LeFevre to murder two of his henchmen. She was nearer now, entering the pool of light from the single overhead light that was burning. She gripped a beret in her right hand and her fiery hair was spilled about her shoulders. She swung the beret in jaunty salute.

"How're you, Commissioner? How's my old pal, Dick Wentworth?"

Both men stood silent, staring at her. Wentworth saw that Detective James' habitual smile had left his face, replaced by a worried frown.

"What happened, Mr. Commissioner?" he asked respectfully. "I just saw her kiting out of the front door and knew she had no business here, so I brought her back."

Kirkpatrick jerked his head. "Bring her downstairs."

"So now you beat up women!" she jeered, but she wasn't frightened. Her saucy nose was wrinkled in amusement. "I warn you I'll show my bruises in court, Kirkpatrick, so be sure to make them where a modest lady can show them without undue blushing."

WENTWORTH DROPPED back where he could walk beside her. James' hand was still clamped tightly on her arm and a smile was tugging at his mouth corners. Margie's humor had its points.

Could this girl be a murderer? Was her hardness more than

49

the shell Wentworth had thought it? He remembered that Nita had been intent on following Margie Huron and wondered if she were outside the building. He hesitated for a moment, then shook his head. If Margie Huron had found out she was being shadowed, she would, supposing she were turned loose again, never lead them to Ricey Charlton.

Kirkpatrick thrust the girl roughly into the pistol range, and she paused, just suppressing a gasp at sight of Strauss, motionless on the floor. She laughed, "Trying to bluff me, Kirkpatrick? Trying to make me think you kill people with your third degree?" She swaggered toward Strauss and all three men dropped back to let her approach alone. There was still a jauntiness to her narrow, virginal back, a defiance in the tilt of her head. She stood over Strauss and stirred him with her toe.

"Come on, Fritzie, get up. You can't fool Margie, the Huron. Get up before I scalp you."

Her second effort disturbed Strauss' arm, which had been thrown across his face. It slid away and thumped to the floor and Margie screamed. She reeled back and beat her thighs with her fists. Detective James started forward, knelt beside Strauss, then turned his drained face upward to stare into Margie Huron's face. Her head began to sway from side to side, her eyes holding his.

"I didn't do it, bandit," she whispered. "I didn't do that. I just sneaked in when I followed the Commissioner here from the Gaillard building. I thought there might be a good story in an expose of a third degree. Honest, that's all it was. *I swear it was!*"

Kirkpatrick's hand went slowly up to part his mustache. He

turned to Wentworth and lifted his shoulders in a slight shrug. "If she hasn't got a gun…" he began.

"I have," Margie said harshly. "You don't think I can go gallivanting around the places the city editor sends me and not carry a gun, do you? Oh, hell…" She stretched out her wrists, "Put them on me, Jesse Bandit Jim."

Kirkpatrick spoke slowly, "Strauss was in with this criminal who calls himself Insanity, Incorporated. He was about to give us valuable information when he was shot. We follow at once and fail to find anyone in the building. You were running from the building and you have a gun. It seems we must at least check its rifling with the bullet that killed Strauss. I suppose you shot it earlier this evening, didn't you, Miss Huron, just for practice?"

Margie Huron's face was white and she struggled hard to make it jaunty again. "I did," she said clearly. "I stopped at the pistol range on Forty-second Street and shot a whole magazine, and the clip I put in was one bullet shy. It's a perfect set-up, Kirkpatrick. The guy at Forty second Street might remember a girl that used her own gun. I hope to hell he does. Otherwise little Margie is apt to leave her scalp in the executioner's hands." She thumped her chest lightly with a fist. "But us Hurons can take it. Lay on, MacDuff." Her arm was a little twisted. "Will the old sheet love this story! I hope they give me a by-line…."

DETECTIVE JAMES had risen methodically to his feet. He took handcuffs from his belt and put them on her wrists that were too small for the bracelets to do much good. He was smiling but not with any amusement at all. Wentworth realized sharply that James was in love with the girl, but that it would

51

not keep him from doing his full duty. He looked to Kirkpatrick for orders.

"Shall I book her in the precinct, or take her to headquarters?" he asked quietly.

Kirkpatrick shook his head. "Take the bracelets off her and let her go. Miss Huron, go to headquarters and surrender your gun and your permit. You don't carry a forty-five, do you, Miss Huron?"

Margie Huron's hands trembled a little as she unfastened her handbag and took out a thirty-two caliber automatic. "All the same to you if I turn this over now? I guess I'm not the woman I thought I was." She held out her wrists to Detective James. "How about a bite to eat and a drop of coffee for a little girl that ain't feeling so hot, bandit?"

Kirkpatrick nodded dismissal to James and when they had gone, he moved swiftly to a telephone, gave crisp orders that the girl was to be followed night and day. "And put two men with a speck of intelligence on the job. The girl is not an imbecile and she might grow suspicious if the men walk on her heels too often." There was an unusual bitterness in his tones.

Wentworth smiled at him, "Would you mind calling headquarters again, Kirk, and telling whoever is to trail Margie that Nita is not a gun moll and that she will be glad to be relieved of the job of following Margie?"

Kirkpatrick stared at him grimly for a few moments, then he grinned. "Then Margaret's presence at your place wasn't as innocent as you indicated to James?"

Wentworth shrugged, "She was of much more service free

than in prison. I'm looking for Ricey Charlton and she's his girl-friend."

While Kirkpatrick telephoned a second time, the sergeant broke in on his orders with a sharp voiced report of disaster. Sudden insanity had stricken a man amid the after-theater crowd on a subway platform. He had hurled nine people to the rails in front of a speeding express train before he had been overpowered by the terrified throng. On Broadway, a man with a powerful limousine had charged into the crowded sidewalks at top speed and had mowed down almost half a hundred persons before his machine jammed on the piled-up bodies. Even then he had not been content, but had struck about him with a heavy wrench until a policeman had shot him down. His name was Francis Fay, a man of great wealth, and in his pocket had been found a threat from Insanity, Inc.

Wentworth and Kirkpatrick stared at each other with a mounting fear. Insanity had been the extortion threat, and men had gone mad—but also had snuffed out scores of innocent lives.

"I'm going to find Nita at once," Wentworth said and heard his own voice queerly muffled. Kirkpatrick nodded and they went together to the street. They found the restaurant in which James and Margie had taken refuge, but there was no trace of Nita. A tingle of alarm ran along Wentworth's nerves. One attempt already had been made upon the woman he loved. LeFevre would not be satisfied with the horror he had wrought in the Spider's home....

Wentworth hurried to a phone, but there was no answer to the long, rhythmic ringing either at his own penthouse or at

Nita's apartment in Riverside Towers. His face was grave with anxiety as he returned to Kirkpatrick.

"She's taken up some new trail," he said flatly. "She must have seen someone she thought she could follow with more profit.

Kirkpatrick nodded. "Yes. Certainly, that's what it is."

Neither man smiled as they hastened to police headquarters. Terror was in their midst and apprehension sat upon their shoulders. Stripped of all his helpers at one swoop, and now Nita....

A curse crowded against Wentworth's teeth. By God, he would run down LeFevre, and when they met... when they met....

CHAPTER 4
TRAIL OF MADNESS

A T POLICE headquarters, Wentworth immediately suggested several methods of tracing LeFevre. No Frenchman, least of all a man of his type, would do without good wines. His *dossier* from *Sûreté de Paris* gave his preference in cigars, dress, drink and women. The police would turn the heat

NITA VAN SLOAN

on Charlton, sending trusted men to every Underworld hideout and lawyer to serve warning that if Charlton were harbored, his benefactors would be the ones to suffer. Kirkpatrick's men would not be too gentle about the warning. Every person who had any connection or acquaintance with Charlton would be watched.

LeFevre had entered the country illegally, probably on a

forged passport, and that put government men on his heels also. Wentworth did not actually hope that any one of these devices would trap LeFevre, but they would make things uncomfortable for him. He would be hampered in all stages of his work and his anger would boil over. Wentworth intended, at that time, to give him an opportunity to boil....

It was late when Wentworth returned to his home. The emptiness mocked him and its untouched disorder was a goad. He went directly to the gymnasium and selected a long-bladed Ferrara rapier. He bent it, tip to hilt, let it swish free, made a few shadow lunges, then held it, balanced, on his palm. There was a pinched look about his mouth. God, yes, he would give LeFevre an opportunity to boil over!

It was well along into the morning when the telephone bell jerked him from an enforced sleep. He was wide awake when his hand touched the instrument.

"Nita!" he cried as her voice came to him, soft and swift, over the wire. He said no more then, for Nita's very tones were a warning.

"Dropped Margie's trail at the Academy," she said swiftly, "to follow a man who ran out of the building ahead of her. They spoke, then he ran. Charlton's man. I'm at..." Her voice broke off with a wild laughter and her voice was blurred as if with drink. "Sure, I know you, Big Shot. Ricey Charlton himself. Last time I saw you was... not three blocks from here at your club. Didn't know you could have a ritzy apartment like this... Since when did they allow mugs like you in the San—"

The phone clicked dead, and automatically Wentworth

56

signaled the operator and demanded a tracer on the phone. Nita had been interrupted in her telephoning, but with her shrewd brain had almost devised a way to tell him. Only Charlton's interference, his disconnecting of the call, had prevented her. Within three blocks of Charlton's club in a high class apartment house whose name began *San... San* what? San Salvador? Santa Clara?

While he waited, Wentworth thumbed swiftly through the phone book to the list of apartment houses. He cursed his shaking hand. If Charlton had seen through Nita's trickery she was in deadly peril! And Charlton might decide to leave the place immediately. How clever was Charlton? Wentworth conceded grimly that the man was pretty smart. He had sensed the doom of prohibition and switched his racket before any other racketeer in the city.

The operator sing-songed: "The call was from a dial telephone, sir. I am sorry that we cannot trace it."

Before she had half completed her message, Wentworth had left the phone and was throwing on his clothing. His dash across the city in his Hispano smashed a dozen traffic rules, but within five minutes, he was in the neighborhood of the club. He bracketed three blocks in each direction from the spot and began a top speed weaving across town. At each apartment house he slowed long enough to spot its name. How long had it been since Nita had phoned him? But he had no conception of the time. Seconds had seemed minutes long in his race to Nita's rescue.

His brakes pulled down the Hispano's long nose and he stared at an apartment house which boasted two doormen. That was the sort of place, with its cheap, imitation Oriental style, that Charlton would pick. Its name... was *Sandalton*. The Hispano ground tires against the curb and before it fairly ceased to roll, Wentworth was striding choppily across the walk. One of the doormen lifted a whistle to his lips and Wentworth sprang wide to his right, deliberately threw himself prone to the pavement and rolled. The first thin note of the whistle was drowned in the thick chatter of a machine gun...!

QUICK AS Wentworth had been, the lead splashed grayly on the pavement within inches of his body as he rolled. There was a sunken stairway and he gathered himself and dived head first into its concrete protection. Not until then did he draw his guns. His face was tight, drawn, not with fear for himself, but for what the ambush indicated. Charlton had penetrated Nita's deception and he had known, either because of her identity or because he had succeeded in tracing the call, whom she had summoned. Nita was not here. That was certain, but her captors would pay a penalty....

The sub-machine gun's blue flicker of powder flame came from a second-story window across the street. Wentworth drew his two automatics deliberately. Two shots were necessary before the gun was silenced, and Wentworth sprang instantly to the sidewalk, darted for the doors of the Sandalton. The doorman who had piped the signal for the blast turned to flee and Wentworth whipped him down with a gun barrel, jerked him over his shoulder as he ran. This man had earned death. He might win it if he did not talk freely at the Spider's command....

The elevator boy tried to slam the door, but a warning shot that piped past his ear on a thin, deadly note changed his mind.

"Charlton's apartment," Wentworth said quietly. "I am expected!"

The operator's eyes could not be narrowed. Tremblings plucked from time to time at his shoulders and legs. When he opened the door, Wentworth thrust him ahead and they went slowly toward a door that had been covered with gold leaf. As they approached, the door whipped back and guns began to speak. Impossible to say how many there were. Lead blasted through that doorway like hurricane blown twigs, thick and fast, and a thousand times more deadly. The bullets cut short the scream that started in the operator's throat, hurled him back against Wentworth's chest and pinned him there, shaking, quivering to the lead which was riddling his body. The Spider felt the dull burn of a bullet that had pierced his human shield and buried himself to the floor. He was not wounded. Probably that shot had not even broken flesh....

In the darkness beyond the open door, Wentworth glimpsed gun flame and fired once. Blackness replaced the flare of shots. He blasted twice more with his automatic and the lights went out in the hall. After that, an aching silence descended on all the building. It lasted for minutes, then from the doorway three guns spoke almost as one. Wentworth held his fire, though not for reasons of safety. The man who could shoot accurately in the darkness, aiming at pistol flashes, was a rarity, for such shooting must be purely by weight and balance of the gun and such knowledge comes only after hours on hours of practice. Wentworth could kill with an easy swiftness in the blackest night, but he did not fire.

He actually leveled his weapon to shoot, but he did not. There was no reason at all. He was impatient with himself and lifted his automatic to wait for the next flash to give him a target. When it came, he did not shoot. Sweat stood out on his forehead abruptly.

He whispered, *"Nita…!"*

There was no response save a storm of lead, some of which plucked into the body behind which he lay. His lips shrank back in a cold anger from his teeth. Noiselessly, he reloaded an almost empty gun; then he writhed forward on his belly across the floor. Inside that room were his enemies, who must die, but it was not they who had put upon him the strange compulsion against shooting… Above his head, the guns continued to speak sporadically. A man whispered to another, "Think we got him, Pete?"

Another man grunted, "Got more lives than a cat. Wish we had a light."

Silence then while Wentworth inched forward, traveling in a straight, unswerving line through the doorway, toward the opposite wall of the room at a spot directly behind the door. This was the spot where his bullets would have hit, had he fired….

The whispering renewed. "What about the dame? Shall I bump her?"

"I'm running this," the other snarled back "Keep your trap shut!"

WENTWORTH LAY motionless, feeling a cold creep up his back. They had a woman prisoner in here. Something like a frenzy seized upon him. He wriggled swiftly forward, hands groping before him. They touched something soft and yielding, yet inert to his pressure, and for an instant, he held his breath. He groped again, identified the rough texture of a man's clothing, found the thick stickiness of blood. He had fired one shot and that bullet had slain. But the woman prisoner, where was she? Who was she?

Wentworth groped past the dead man and his hand touched a slim ankle clad in silk. He felt a tremor touched the leg and released it, got carefully first to his knees, then to his feet while his hands moved lightly to discover the woman's bonds. There were ropes about her wrists and arms, about her throat, holding her rigid against a half open door. There was a gag….

His fingers brushed her hair and a tingling thrill shot through him. Hair like that, as soft and downy as virgin silk. He leaped so close his lips touched her ear. He was trembling, too, trembling with the immensity of his discovery, with the horror of the thing that had almost happened in the darkness and which only some strange psychic bond had prevented….

"It's Dick, Nita love!" he whispered, heard her breath gust out in relief.

"Hey, Pete, you hear anything?" the restless man whispered.

"Yeah, you!" the man hissed back. "Shut your trap. Get your light out and take a look at the hall. Somebody might have heard us in the street and called the cops."

Wentworth's pocket knife sliced rope after rope, but he held them carefully from falling. He freed the gag last, drew Nita gently into the closet, to the door of which she had been tied.

He was vibrant with what was a cross between fear and anger. He had been as close as that in the darkness to... *to killing Nita!*

There could be no doubt about it. The man in the streets had not been intended to hit him with machine-gun bullets. He knew that now, for the whistle signal had been too obvious, too blatant. Nor had he been intended to die here in the hall until his bullets had first slain Nita. She was their trump card. He knew without question that, if they had failed to kill him here in the hall, they would have thrown a light upon Nita and planned to slay him while, stricken with horror, he gazed upon the dead body of the woman he loved. They had even, he perceived, placed a man to fire from behind the door to which she was tied, so that he would have a good target. But his skill had been equal even to that. When his lead had sped, it had been absolutely true. He had hit the man behind the gun, not erring by so much as the few inches which would have meant Nita's death!

Wentworth felt more than thought these things, for his senses were alert upon the men about him. Though be had snatched Nita from her perilous position, they were by no means safe....

The flashlight speared into the hall as the man called Pete had instructed, revealed the dead elevator operator, but nothing more. With a hoarse shout, men thronged to the door, five of them packed into a close knot. Wentworth thrust Nita behind him into the closet, lifted his two guns on his palms. Then he laughed the flat, mocking laughter, sinister as death, which men had heard before this in the hour of their death, the laughter of the Spider!

The grouped men whirled in frozen terror and the Spider's

guns began a swift, deadly rhythm. It was over in an instant, the time it would take to fire five bullets from the deadly twin throats of Wentworth's automatics. Only one of the five murderers fired an answering shot. The flashlight flew high into the air, turning in a slow somersault, its crazy beam flashing in the death agony of men before it struck and crashed into darkness. Wentworth swept Nita into his arms and sped from the building. He was three blocks away before he remembered that he should have allowed one man to live for a while. Dead men can't talk....

YET WENTWORTH was cheerful as he returned to his penthouse. He had struck a heavy blow at his enemy and Nita was safe again. They repaired to the kitchen and Nita refused to sit down and let him make the arrangements. She laughed. "It was much more of an ordeal for you than for me," she told him. "All I had to do was die..." Her deep violet eyes held his steadily through long seconds. "Dick, why didn't you shoot except just that once?"

Wentworth smiled gently, took her in his arms. "I got your message," he said. "Ram Singh says that your soul and mine, our *karma*, is one!"

Nita laughed comfortably. "That's silly," she said. "You just guessed that there might be a reason why they opened the door so wide to shoot at you!"

Wentworth shrugged and, at her insistence, dropped into a chair while she moved deftly about the small kitchen. A mighty longing rose within him, but he put it angrily down. Surely, that all was done with long ago. The Spider could not marry. What would a childless marriage be? And how could a man in deadly

peril of the law expose his loved ones to that overwhelming disgrace…? Wentworth shook himself, but his eyes followed Nita's graceful figure as she went happily about her work. Nita glanced toward him and shook her head.

Wentworth's cane snapped against
one gunman's jaw; the other he hurled
headlong into Tyson's belly!

"Dick, you know you wouldn't be satisfied in a cottage for two. You'd have to shave yourself and lay out your own clothes and…."

Wentworth said, more gravely than usual, "Don't tease me, Nita."

Her smile vanished and she turned swiftly back to the making of some sandwiches. The kettle began to sing on the stove. Nita turned toward it, popping a piece of cheese into her mouth.

"I just can't wait!" she cried like a little girl, her mouth full. "I didn't eat any supper."

She poured hot water into the teapot, teetered back in a chair. "No, Dick, not a bite until the tea is ready."

Wentworth grinned as she slapped his hands away from the sandwiches and resolutely thrust grim thoughts from his brain. Such moments as these were far too rare to be sullied by worries and despair. Just he and Nita....

He reached for her hand and Nita started abruptly to her feet, stiffened hand pressing to her temple.

"Dick!" she whispered. "Dick... my... brain...!"

Wentworth jerked from the chair, a wild fear stabbing at his heart, "Nita...?" He reached for her, but she dodged from under his hands. She sprang across the kitchen and her hand closed eagerly about a long, thin-bladed knife. As Wentworth rushed toward her, she whirled and struck out at him viciously.

Only Wentworth's life of desperate action enabled him to dodge that strong, sure blow. He flinched aside, stumbled, pitched to the floor. As he fell, Nita's face came strongly into the light. It was warped from all semblance of its normal sweetness and her eyes stared wildly. There was white foam on her lips. With a shrill eerie laugh, she sprang upon Wentworth and slashed downward murderously with the knife! A frenzied moan rose to Wentworth's lips as he lifted numb hands to ward away the blow. Nita, his Nita...! *She was quite insane!*

CHAPTER 5
THE SPIDER'S GUNS

THE SHOCK of Nita's madness almost cost Wentworth's life. His hands were leaden as they moved to parry the knife and it slashed past within an inch of his throat to stab into the floor.

"Nita!" he gasped. "For God's sake, *Nita!*" Even as he pleaded, he knew the words were worse than useless. If Nita's mind were to be reached by anything he were to say or do, that knife would never have thirsted for his throat....

The very savagery of the blow defeated Nita's mad purpose. Deeply embedded in the flooring, the knife resisted Nita's struggle to tug it free and during those few swift seconds of respite, Wentworth's keen brain rallied. He pinioned Nita's arms in his powerful embrace and holding her close to him, staggered erect.

It was hard to use force against Nita, to exert his mighty strength against the woman he loved, but no mild measures would subdue her. She fought with all the savage cunning that the Spider had taught, gnashing with her white, fine teeth and striking with her knees and the spikes of her heels.

Though he realized its uselessness, Wentworth pleaded with her while he struggled, begged her to stop, to rest... God, this was unbearable, this sudden madness... Wentworth felt that his sanity would snap under the strain. Nita was insane, he suddenly understood, *because she had been the first to taste the food!*

He remembered how she had driven his hands playfully from the snack she prepared. And her recognition of the confusion of her brain had been instantaneous. At the expense of her own sweet self, Nita had saved him…!

A great wave of weariness and an aching pain flooded Wentworth as he carried Nita, still struggling violently, to a bed and bound her helpless with wide bands from blankets. He stood looking down at her impotent rage throughout long moments of black despair. He was conscious, too, that another emotion now fought in him for supremacy—a small, hot point of fury that swelled within him! One man was responsible for this— one man who had sent desolation into a score of homes, whose maniac victims had killed in the frenzy produced by his drugs. Now he had reached into Wentworth's home for the second time—and even more terribly than that first…!

Wentworth's clenched fists lifted, shaking above his head. By the gods, the Spider would have full vengeance! He would sweep this malefactor from the face of the earth; he would…!

Wentworth's hands lowered impotently. Unbridled anger would gain him nothing. He had been unable to trace even one of the LeFevre's lesser minions. Unless he could do that, unless he could get a clue, his anger was worse than useless and became merely the vaporings of a madman….

He dared not leave Nita alone, lest she harm herself or break free and stalk him. His hand moved woodenly toward the telephone and, briefly, he summoned Sam Higgens, his doctor, to bring nurses and care for Nita. Before this, Higgens had served the Spider. He owed him much and he did not hesitate to obey. A few minutes later he strode in with brisk, characteristic efficiency, palming his stiff red hair to his scalp and resolutely ignoring Wentworth's pain.

"All right, all right!" he said sharply. "Get out. Leave her to me. Get out, I say…!"

Long after the doctor had arrived, Wentworth delayed his departure. He knew it was useless to linger here, but his heart was so torn that it seemed impossible to turn his mind toward the battle which lay ahead. He sat at the foot of the bed and stared into Nita's distorted face. His sounds were mostly inarticulate, but full of rage. There was froth about the sweet lips he had kissed. He jerked to his feet, pounded from the room. If ever he had needed a goad for his duty, certainly he had it now! There was nothing he could do here more than was already being done. His very presence seemed to rouse Nita to new furies.

He realized abruptly that even the experiments to discover what drugs had been put in the food could be better handled by the cool, experienced hands of Sam Higgens. The doctor had pledged his word not to leave the apartment until he had effected a cure or until Wentworth himself bade him go… But that latter was a possibility they did not mention. Finally, Wentworth forced himself to depart….

HE WAS still utterly without a clue to LeFevre's whereabouts nor did he hope to discover immediately where Ricey Charlton had fled, but there was some thing the Spider could do, and all the heated urgency of Wentworth's blood drove him on.

Charlton had many allies. Two leaders in the rackets especially had bound themselves to him. Dutch Tyson and Paul Collins, known better as the Bouncer. If they did not know where Charlton was, at least they would have some means of communication. It was true that they might be more than reluctant to give that information to the Spider... Wentworth's lips drew back, thin and bitter, from his teeth. The Spider had met... and conquered... reluctance... before this!

Wentworth struggled, with these new thoughts, to banish the awful memory of Nita's condition from his brain. He must achieve, before he first challenged the gangsters, the complete unity of purpose, the utter readiness of thought that must be his when he went into danger and action. It was this capacity for whole minded concentration, as much as any other single thing, which had made the Spider the one overwhelming menace which the Underworld feared! But the mood would not come. It would not....

Perspiration beaded out now on Wentworth's forehead with his effort at absolute control and he was still white and shaken when his taxi dropped him before the storage garage where he knew Dutch Tyson made his headquarters.

There was no need for concealment, as there would be if he had worn the garb of the Spider, and tonight, it must be clearly Wentworth who challenged, for it was to Wentworth that LeFevre had carried the fiendish warfare. So he strolled openly across the broad walk toward the garage office, swinging his sword-cane jauntily. Within the office, a man lounged lazily in a swivel chair, his fingers laced across a fat-swollen abdomen.

He glanced up with a carelessness which was three quarters studied insolence.

"And what might you want, buddy?" the man demanded.

Wentworth still appeared casual, yet his fist moved so swiftly it blurred as he caught the man's shirt in a tight knot beneath his chin. There was a single, smooth ripple of movement and the man was swung across the room, released just when his whirling body reached its fullest momentum, sent reeling backward through the door and onto the auto ramp that slanted upward into the building. The fat man lost his balance, flopped heavily and his feet kicked helplessly in the air. Wentworth stood just clear of his frantically flailing feet and spoke with a suave quietness which was strangely at variance with his lightning attack.

"You may tell Dutch Tyson," he announced pleasantly, "that Richard Wentworth is calling."

A gun glinted now in the hand of the fallen man and Wentworth had scarcely seemed to notice it. Nevertheless, his cane licked out with the drive and violence of a rapier lunge and the gun clattered across the concrete. The man whimpered over his cracked wrist.

"I gave you a message," the Spider reminded him. "Must I wait longer?"

Wentworth felt a fierce exultation. He was not a man who gloated in pain, but he himself had been fearfully hurt and he was striking back at those who had brought this awful suffering to him and Nita....

He stood, very quietly, peering with an almost benevolent smile at the man he had vanquished. If he knew that, from the shadows of the upper ramp, another gunman covered him, he gave absolutely no indication. He moved the cane slightly and the fat man flinched to his feet and cringed, whimpering for mercy. At a gesture, he slunk away up the ramp with Wentworth in his wake. Wentworth strove to calm himself. He knew that he should have used more caution in invading the sanctum of a killer. But it was not in him tonight to be careful....

The gunman who had covered him from the shadows of the ramp was not in sight when Wentworth prodded his terrified guide past the spot. But the Spider knew that a dark, furtive shape followed as they moved higher and higher into the building. He knew and did not care. Enemies were before him and behind him—men who would not hesitate to kill one they hated and feared so fiercely as Wentworth, even without the further provocation he intended to give.

He paused and called out: "Come out of hiding, Tyson. I promise not to hurt you... right away!"

AT FIRST, only his echo answered him, then brilliant light from overhead dazzled him and, in the momentary blindness, his fleshy guide fled. It would have been simple to follow those fleeing footsteps with a bullet, but Wentworth had come for far bigger game....

"What's the matter, Tyson? Didn't I promise not to hurt you... right away?"

A heavy fire-door which had been standing open slid into a closed position to reveal a dark aperture behind its old resting place. Within that false doorway, nothing was visible, but from it a voice came to Wentworth's ears clearly:

"I don't need your promises, Wentworth. Come in, but don't try any funny business."

Wentworth laughed and there was a queer, fierce joy in the sound. Confidently, but without swagger, he strolled through the doorway and, as he passed, felt the hard muzzles of two guns dig into his loins.

"No funny business!" a hoarse, excited voice warned.

"Don't you try anything at all," a second echoed and a shove of a gun muzzle put an exclamation point on each phrase.

Wentworth made no answer and his silence fell upon his captors, weighed upon them like heavy burdens. Finally a door opened ahead and, now inside, Wentworth leaned jauntily on the head of his sword-cane. He was, he saw, in the sanctum of Dutch Tyson, fitted up more as a luxurious lounge-room than a racketeer's office. One wall shone richly with the varied bindings of expensive books and a sportsman's arsenal of guns was stacked against another. The casualness which always marked the Spider when he was most dangerous, sat upon his shoulders now like a fashionable cloak.

"Nice books," he murmured, with an amicable gesture.

Dutch Tyson looked at him very steadily and nodded twice. "Yes, they're nice. Paid almost a month's take for them." His voice was even, monotonous.

"Nice guns, too."

Tyson merely nodded this time.

"A rare man," Wentworth suggested, still murmuring, "who can combine the taste for fine literature with the more active life of a sportsman."

73

Dutch Tyson continued to stare at him with black, unblinking eyes. "Listen, bo," he said sharply, "I've got things to do. Suppose you talk."

"Suppose you talk," Wentworth countered persuasively. "Otherwise, I shall find it necessary to blow that fat little belly of yours to bits!"

That brought Tyson to his feet with a congested, purpling face. "You… you…!" He waved his heavy, club like arms. "You…!"

"You said that before," Wentworth reminded him pleasantly. "What I want to know is really very simple. *Where… is… Ricey… Charlton?*" His voice was little more than a whisper, yet the words hung like tangible fearful threats in the air.

Tyson rolled his heavy shoulder forward. "You damned fool," he said pityingly. "You poor damned fool!" He moved a thick hand in what was obviously a signal and Wentworth went into action with the smooth and effortless efficiency of a streamlined train. As he stepped backward, his right hand, gripping the cane just below its head, snapped against one gunman's jaw. His left hand, gripping a nape that had too much hair, hurled its owner head-first into Tyson's belly. Those two collapsed to the floor and when they could look up again, it was upon the shining, gray steel of Wentworth's sword, so close it seemed to burn their throats. Behind it were two blue-gray eyes which held a light as keen and menacing as the rapier's needle point. Wentworth was laughing, laughing….

"Will you talk now, Dutch," he inquired politely, "or shall I start slicing your home grown belly into bacon strips? *Where… is… Ricey… Charlton?*"

Tyson's face had been gray before; now it became bloodless.

"I don't know," he whispered. "I don't *know!* As God is my witness, I *don't know!* Don't stick me with that sword again. It...*Ahrr!*"

"Now, now, Dutch," Wentworth soothed. "I gave you no more than a quarter-inch of the blade. I..." His attention seemed wholly on the two before him and yet, behind him, he caught the click of a revolver hammer being cocked. He slashed the honed point of the rapier behind him with a skilled assurance that did not even require him to turn his head about.

Afterward, he continued to stare into Tyson's eyes and saw there things he could read only in sounds, in the scream that was thin with unnerving pain and abject terror.

"Dutch...?" Wentworth began questioningly.

The man groveled. The fat of his whole body quivered and the chattering of his teeth made what he said the maunderings of an idiot. He was begging, pleading....

WENTWORTH STOOD, rigid and merciless as stone, while the scream behind him died to a whimpering moan, to a rough, strangled breathing—to the silence of death. Wentworth's eyes were narrower. Tyson was overdoing this fear business a little. Wentworth knew that he was notoriously yellow, but such an abject coward as this man showed himself now would never have survived the rigors of prohibition gangsterism. Realization of that fact was more intuition than deliberation, as was his decision that Tyson was in some way baiting a clever trap for him....

Wentworth spun about, saw that his mind's warning had

already come instants too late. He was covered by a machine gun held by the fat man with the injured wrist. The killer was crouched over his weapon, his whole body avid for the kill, a trembling forefinger on the trigger, tense with the desire to slaughter. Tyson's voice grated out terribly.

"What in the hell are you waiting for? Burn him down! *Burn him down!*" Dutch Tyson screamed shrilly.

Death stared Wentworth in the face. There wasn't one chance in ten that he could reach the machine gunner before he loosed hot lead from its muzzle. He must take that chance, of course. Even before his body had completed the maneuver of turning, he had made up his mind how he must strike. With the momentum of his turn, he sent the rapier flashing, point-first, toward the machine gunner's throat. If the man held his ground, the feint could not possibly save Wentworth's life. But he must gamble on the deadly sword causing the fat kneeling gunner to flinch. The man hunched forward, ducking under the blade, eyes blazing on Wentworth. His finger tightened… and he died. That single blast of a gun had not been the weapon in his hands, but another, off there in the darkness of the garage. His head snapped over on his right shoulder. The instantaneous bright gush of blood stained his shirt. Wentworth waited for no more than that. Help had come from some unexpected quarter. He threw himself to the floor, snatching out his twin automatics in a swift double cross-draw, faced his living enemies. He was not a moment too soon. As his glance returned to Dutch Tyson and his bodyguard, the men's guns snapped into their hands. There was a blended roar of convulsing guns and Wentworth scrambled to his feet. Tyson and his guard did not. They never would rise again....

Within a space of seconds, Wentworth clicked the room into darkness and reached the door where the machine gunner had died. From the movement of the slain man's head, he had been shot from the right along this corridor. He peered cautiously into it. Fifty feet away, dim light slanted across the hallway. It revealed no movement at all, no blotched shadow that might be a man. Nevertheless, Wentworth sped along it with utmost caution. There was a deep frown on his forehead. Someone had killed the machine gunner in the last split-second of time to save Wentworth's life. And yet now, no more than a half-minute later, the long corridor was empty. Nor did he encounter anyone in his swift descent of the ramps to the street. He stood a half-minute in the shadow of the building, peering closely, about him. In all the dark vista, nothing moved that might be human. Wentworth moved his shoulders jerkily. Silly to feel apprehensive over the fact that his life had been saved, and yet that was his reaction. The shooting of the machine gunner at that precise moment could not be coincidental. It followed that some one, friendly to the Spider, had struck a blow in his behalf.

Wentworth laughed shortly and strode up the street toward a taxi stand he knew to be three blocks away. "Thanks, friend!" he called softly into the darkness. He kept a sharp look-out, but he discovered no trace of anyone on his trail. It intrigued him, but grimly he pressed on about his business. Overconfidence had lost him his opportunity to make Dutch Tyson betray Charlton, but there was still another opportunity. Paul Collins was even closer to the racketeer the Spider sought, but this time he must plan his action in advance. This time, there must be no slip-up, or Charlton would slip his clutches, and there would be no other way of reaching LeFevre....

COLLINS WAS a smarter, smoother man than Tyson, and more deadly. Gambling furnished him an elaborate livelihood. Not that he ever sat at a green baize table unless for pleasure. His was the money, the protection behind three major gaming houses which were placed strategically in the richest sections of the city. The nearest approach he had to a direct connection with any one of them was to have an apartment in the same building in which the Park Avenue "house" was situated. And some two hundred other people shared that connection....

The taxi driver glanced at Wentworth shrewdly as he gave the address. "That's a soup-and-fish joint, mister," he explained sociably. "Even the bell-boys wear tails."

Wentworth said, "I'm in a hurry." The driver muscled the cab out from the curb and got under way fast, but his fare's attention left him instantly, concentrated on the back trail. However, he saw no signs of surveillance. He shifted restlessly. He was mad to think that anyone had interfered in his behalf. Everyone in any way connected with him had fallen victim to LeFevre.... At the Marguerite, the doorman did look askance at his clothing, but there was no such impertinence within. There was that in Wentworth's bearing which did not admit of challenge. He went directly to the elevators, frowning a little. Perhaps it would have been better to have himself announced. He intended to enter Collin's apartments openly. His plans were laid....

The operator of the cage stared openly when he mentioned Collins' floor. "Mr. Collins prefers to have his callers announced," he said flatly.

Wentworth permitted his gaze to touch the operator and the man saluted, "I beg your pardon, sir. It's only that Mr. Collins gave us all such strict instructions."

Wentworth nodded carelessly. The elevator doors opened into a handsomely furnished reception room and beyond curtained doorways, Wentworth could see the drawing-room. A butler whose eyes held the cold glitter of men who kill stepped stiffly forward and did not offer to take hat or cane. His eyes followed each movement as Wentworth fingered a card from his waist-coat pocket.

The butler looked at the card, his glance flew back to Wentworth's face and a faint color touched his cheek-bones. He did not leave the reception-room but summoned a second butler to carry the card inside. His gaze did not leave Wentworth, and slight amusement touched the Spider's lips... He was instantly aware when Collins came presently to the doorway through which the second butler had vanished, but he allowed several seconds to elapse before he turned casually that way. Collins came forward suavely, holding out his hand.

"An unexpected pleasure, but a genuine one, nevertheless," he said equably. He was dressed in the height of formal fashion. His studs were black pearls and in excellent taste. His rather thick lips were parted in a smile, though his eyes held a cold gleam which Wentworth recognized. "Come in! Come in!" Collins cried.

WENTWORTH BOWED, tucked his hat and cane under his left arm to accept Collins' proffered hand. "I won't detain you long from your friends," he said quietly. "I only wish to be directed or taken to Ricey Charlton."

"Haven't seen him for weeks," Collins shook his head. "But come in and I'll see what I can find out." He led Wentworth

through the living-room where he introduced him to two men and three women, two of whom he identified. Phyllis March had been married a little over a year and her husband's fortune was in the millions. Phyllis was a little drunk. The other was Dorsey Hayrol, who had been a debutante the year before. Strange company for a racketeer. Wentworth could see that Collins enjoyed the introductions… He bustled toward a smaller room that opened with a massive door from the main hall.

"My study," he murmured. "Some time when you're unhurried, I'd like you to inspect my library."

Wentworth glanced at the shelves, more elaborately filled than those of Dutch Tyson. Strange how these men sought to assume a veneer of culture—men who earned their living with blood and murder.…

Collins seated Wentworth solicitously and went to take a telephone from a cover made from a split globe of the world. He was all geniality and smiling friendliness. It was his very ability to play this game which had raised him above the ordinary run of criminals, Wentworth realized, and that fact gave him a new estimate of Ricey Charlton. Charlton was this man's master, and beyond him was LeFevre and, over him, probably, still another. But, Wentworth told himself impatiently, he did not need these proofs of the strength and cleverness of his ultimate adversary. A foe who could strike so venomously at the Spider.…

Without conscious effort, Wentworth memorized the number Collins called. The man's smooth voice interrupted his thoughts. "Collins speaking." He laughed. "Tomorrow and tomorrow and tomorrow, they all go the same way, John. My health remains boringly monotonous. I'm trying to locate Ricey Charlton for a friend. For whom?" He lifted his brows toward Wentworth. "Do you object to my telling your name?"

Wentworth shook his head, smiling. It was all working out perfectly according to plan. He need only wait until he was sure that Collins had made complete arrangements and escorted him from the Marguerite. He had no doubt at all that Collins would go with him, but if he didn't, Wentworth had certain arguments to present. The weight of his automatics beneath his arms was reassuring....

Collins required ten minutes and three phone calls to make the arrangements. Then he rose briskly. "If you don't object, I'll take you to Charlton. You realize, of course, that he is being hunted by the police and he must take certain precautions... I'll just make my apologies."

As he strode past Wentworth toward the door, Wentworth's hand shot out and rigid fingers jabbed certain nerve centers in the throat. He caught Collins as the man lunged, unconscious, toward the floor. Working it this way made his task more laborious, of course, but it would be simpler in the long run....

CHAPTER 6
TRAIL TO DESPAIR

THE CHANGE that Wentworth made then required almost a half hour. With a small pocket make-up kit, he altered both his own and the unconscious Collins' face so that, when the Spider had donned Collins' evening dress, he and the man on the floor had switched identities. The exchange was facilitated by a certain basic resemblance in body and facial contour. Collins' slightly lighter hair had been darkened quickly with a pomade.

While Collins still lay on the floor, Wentworth summoned the butler by bell, gave him curt instructions that the unconscious man, apparently himself, be carried secretly to his car; that the car should pick him up at the front door within five minutes. He bent over Collins again and, under the cover of feeling the pulse, renewed pressure on the nerve centers so that the gambler would remain unconscious for a sufficient length of time. He hurried out of the study then, smiling in Collins' best manner.

"I'm so sorry," he cried, "but I find that I'll have to leave you. Business will obtrude. I hope you won't mind?" It was very apparent that the ladies did, but they accepted his apologies and parted within a few minutes. The rest of the arrangements were easy. The unconscious Collins was carried out of the study and down the service elevator—which, apparently, was manipulated by Collins' own man and, within an hour of his first entry, Wentworth was driving away again....

When Collins, seated beside Wentworth, came back to his senses, he heard Wentworth's voice. "I think you're entirely right about Charlton. He did rather overstep himself in that last killing. None of my business, of course."

Wentworth was watching him narrowly. There was no reason why Collins should know how he had been rendered unconscious, or even that he had lost consciousness. To be sure, there would be a blank in his memory. It was up to Wentworth to convince him that it was exclusively that....

"I know it's imprudent of me, but I can't help telling you again. I can't see how you could have come to throw in with Charlton. You're strong enough in your own right."

Collins stared at him piercingly, looked out at the street whirling past, glanced sharply at the driver and apparently was reassured. It was his car. "The funniest thing," he said uncertainly. "Do you know I have no memory at all of getting into this car?"

Wentworth saw that he was going to succeed with his deception. In the darkness of the car, Collins would not notice that Wentworth had traded faces with him. He might notice that he no longer wore formal dress, but Wentworth had taken pains that his own garments should be hidden beneath the cloak he wore, that his silk hat should rest out of sight....

The car wound about innumerable corners and finally came to a halt within two blocks of Pennsylvania Station, but in a neighborhood that was utterly squalid. As he alighted, Wentworth murmured so that the driver wouldn't hear. "Shall we keep the car?"

Collins nodded, "Better wait."

The driver saluted, hearing his master's voice say he was to remain, not seeing which man had spoken. Collins led the way across the pavement into a sour hallway. He went into a door to his left without knocking, walked directly across the empty room he revealed and began pressing pieces of wooden paneling in the far wall. He stepped back presently and the section of the wall swung out as a door. Wentworth hurled Collins through the opening, presented a pistol at his back.

"There you are, my dear Wentworth," he said pleasantly, assuming Collins' studied suavity. "You can't say that I didn't keep my promise to bring you to Charlton."

COLLINS SPRANG to his feet and, for the first time, saw Wentworth's face in a clear light. He reeled back, his hands flying to his own face. Anger distorted it. He reached out a trembling hand.

"You trickster!" he shouted. "Trying to make them think that you're me!"

The gunman who stood beside the door, weapon in hand, guffawed deeply. "What the hell? Is he gone nuts?"

"Not yet," Wentworth drawled pleasantly, "but I imagine that something of the sort is in store for him."

A rear door of the room in which they stood swung open and Wentworth recognized at once, the long, angular face of Ricey Charlton. There was something of the actor about him even after so many criminal years had intervened between him and the stage. He decidedly "made an entrance," and there was staginess in the way he stood beside the door, tapping a cigarette on a richly embossed case.

Collins ran toward him. "For God's sake, Charlie!" he shouted. "Don't let Wentworth get away with this trick!" He thrust a pointing hand towards Wentworth. "That's him there! That's Wentworth. He's made up to look like me!"

Wentworth smiled slightly at Charlton and Charlton shook his head. He cut Collins' face with a corner of the cigarette case, whipping it in a vicious arc. Collins reeled back, made a hoarse sound that was half moan, half shout.

"For God's sake, Charlton!" he begged.

Ricey Charlton smiled slowly. His voice was deeply resonant. "You have a reputation for cleverness, Wentworth. See if you can't think up a better stall than this one." He waited with an air of polite attention. Collins gouged at his own cheeks, trying to

Wentworth's right crossed to James' jaw with all the impetus of the leap behind it!

remove the make-up, but Wentworth had used indelible preparations of his own formula which could be removed by nothing less than theatrical cold cream.

Wentworth was very much at ease in appearance, but behind his casual manner, his brain raced with plans. Except for Collins, there were only Charlton and his gunman in the room. It would be very simple to crush their lives out, to leave them with the bloody splotch of the Spider's seal on their forehead, but it might be possible to accomplish more than mere death. It was a long, dim trail that he followed, but he had gained a very important victory in forcing his way through to Charlton. Could he not, in the same way, reach LeFevre, and through him…? It was necessary to talk.

"Wentworth had the nerve to come deliberately to you, Charlton," Wentworth said calmly. "He asked me to get in touch, then came along like a little lamb. Does he think we're complete suckers?"

Charlton's muscles jerked. "You were followed, fool!" he shouted. "He put himself in our power so that his friends could follow him…."

Wentworth smiled. "What friends?" he asked gently. "His men are in the hospital…."

"The police!"

Wentworth shook his head. "That may have been his idea, but if we were followed, we shook them off." A fleeting memory touched his mind. Had he been followed by the person who had saved his life in the garage of Dutch Tyson? He shrugged his shoulders. "No, Charlton, I was not followed…" He gazed placidly at the disguised Collins. "What shall we do with him?" He took a few sauntering steps forward. He could not continue the imposture indefinitely. Sooner or later, Collins' stunned mind would begin to function again and he would think of a hundred ways of proving his identity. Before that time, Wentworth must be prepared to eliminate all enemies in one smooth piece of action. He did not want to kill Charlton—that was definite in his mind—for Charlton held the key to the whole mad plot against humanity... His new position put him within striking distance of the gun-guard. It would be better if he forced the issue before Charlton's suspicions were aroused.

"LeFevre would enjoy this," he suggested tentatively and saw from Charlton's frown that the idea was unwelcome. He would not learn, then, where LeFevre was by anything less, than a forced confession.

"We'll let LeFevre do his work," Charlton said shortly. "We'll do ours. Wentworth, will you honor us by a little drink before we consign you to the grave?"

THE DISGUISED Collins started forward eagerly and Wentworth saw that he had recovered from his stunned surprise, that his mind was working on the effort to convince Charlton. "Now!" he cried. "I can prove I'm not Wentworth. Would Wentworth know the trick of the decanter? Would he know that the insanity drug can be released by breaking the vacuum of its container, and...?"

Wentworth waited for no more. His cane leaped high and knocked the gun guard unconscious to the floor. He sprang forward, felling Collins with a second thrust which caught the gang leader beneath the ear. He faced Ricey Charlton, gun in hand, and bowed to him politely.

"It was a question of how long the imposture could continue," Wentworth said quietly. "You'll come with me, please. Don't make it necessary for me to... exert pressure."

For seconds, the rage that scourged Charlton twisted his angular face harshly, but he rapidly regained control, met Wentworth's half-quizzical smile with a satirical bow.

"Allow me to compliment you on your art, Wentworth," he said. "You had me completely fooled. I won't resist, of course...." His voice was entirely calm and, though he surrendered verbally, he made no move to go toward the secret door which Wentworth indicated with a jerk of his head. It became apparent that he was delaying for some reason which Wentworth did not comprehend. Wentworth edged to the wall and got his shoulders against it. His heavy gun jutted forward.

"To the door, Charlton," he said, his voice roughening. "At once!"

Charlton shrugged, moved leisurely across in front of the Spider's ready gun toward the indicated exit. Abruptly, the door by which Charlton had entered whipped open. Wentworth's gun arm pivoted against his hip, the weapon swung smoothly on this new target... and he did not shoot. He took a quick stride forward, checked because he had to. It was that or go down before the gun held by the woman who stood in the doorway—a woman who crouched forward eagerly over her compact automatic, brown eyes shining with excitement.

"Just stand there very carefully," she said, "and I won't have to shoot you. And I can shoot, my friend. I can shoot! I spent a whole dollar tonight just to practice up a bit on a range. Charlie, maybe you better get behind me...."

Wentworth clicked his heels and bowed. "Miss Huron, you always turn up at the most inopportune moments...!"

If he had hoped to disconcert her by speaking in his natural tone, by revealing his identity as Richard Wentworth, he miscalculated on Margie Huron's coolness. She held matters neatly in her small, pink palm. Wentworth could threaten to shoot Charlton, but short of doing that, he couldn't stop the man from his swift progress across the room. If he did shoot Charlton, he himself would be shot to shreds within the next few seconds. Strangely, he did not doubt that Margie Huron would shoot— and shoot to kill—at the least necessity. Yet he could not bring himself to fire on her. The Spider had come to grips with criminal women before, but never, in his long career, had he found it necessary to kill one. His innate chivalry rebelled at the thought, though he knew that, were that act essential to the destruction of some criminal giant, he would not hesitate... But Margie was not basically bad. Women could do mighty things for love, and their capacity for sacrifice often seemed all out of proportion to the worth of the man....

WENTWORTH WAS keenly balanced, though he seemed at ease. If Margie's concentration wavered for an instant... Charlton's darkly handsome face was twisted into a hard sneer as he crouched warily behind the girl... Abruptly, his face whitened. He leaped backward, slammed the door shut and Margie's eyes flicked over Wentworth's shoulder. It was the instant for which he had waited. Regardless now of what new danger threatened from the rear, this was his cue to strike. He lunged forward in a long, low dive, saw that Margie had not turned to run, but that, instead, her gun had sagged to her side. Too late, she became aware of Wentworth's attack, and even then, her resistance was half-hearted....

Wentworth's shoulder caught her knees and together they fell to the floor. He was up instantly, snatching at the knob of the door through which Charlton had vanished.

"Get your hands up!" a man's voice ordered harshly.

The door was locked and Wentworth cursed and wheeled about. Detective Jesse James stood in the other entrance.

"Quickly," Wentworth shouted. "Charlton is escaping from the building! Get out front...."

James' face was drawn and there was a whiteness about his mirthless smile. He was looking at Margie, rather than Wentworth. Margie snickered. "Honest, Bandit, we were just practicing for our wrestling match in the Garden tomorrow night. Did you like it, or didn't I groan in the right tone of voice?" She laughed again, but to Wentworth's ears, the sound was shaky. He jerked his head impatiently.

"For heaven's sake, James," he cried. "I tell you that Charlton is getting away. Don't you recognize my voice? I'm Wentworth..." He took a step forward.

James tilted up his gun muzzle threateningly and Wentworth dropped back. He set his teeth together. James must have seen Charlton escaping. Margie was talking, chattering, as women do to cover up embarrassment, to hide their emotions. "This ain't me either, Bandit. I'm somebody else. Haven't just made up my mind who!" Wentworth glanced at her impatiently, saw that she was patting her abundant red hair into place under a ridiculously small hat. She rose lithely to her feet, put a hand to her back and groaned. "Don't play so rough next time, Collins, me lad."

Wentworth felt desperation rise within him. Damn it, Charlton would get away clean. Detective James was speaking now, his voice harshly broken, but he was slow, slow... Wentworth inched forward, sliding his feet fractions of an inch at a time. He raced at James, knowing that James scarcely heard him.

"You're going to jail," James was telling Margie curtly, "and you'll stay there plenty long. You've tricked me for the last time, and...."

Wentworth sprang to the attack. James caught a glimpse of his first movement and jerked his gun about but Wentworth's fist caught it and knocked it aside. Even then, a quick shot might have scored, but there was also an excellent chance that the bullet would hit Margie. James hesitated to shoot and his chance was gone. Wentworth's right crossed to the jaw with all the impetus of his leap behind it and James swung about, bounced his shoulders mightily against the wall and went down with all his joints going lax.

Wentworth did not wait to disarm him, or even to pickup his own second weapon. He bounded across the room and through the secret door, reached the street and whipped back into the next building, which was the one through which Charlton must have fled. For five, ten minutes, he raged through the tenement and searched the alleyways and basement, but he had known in advance that it was practically hopeless. Charlton had had at least five minutes start... With bitterness in his heart, Wentworth went heavily back to the room in which he had overcome the detective. The girl would be gone, of course, and he would not find her again. She would go into hiding with Charlton....

IN THE doorway, he stopped in his tracks, staring incredulously into the room. Margie Huron was still there. Seated on the floor, she had lifted James' head and shoulders into her lap and she crooned over him as if he were a baby, swaying back and forth. She was making no attempt to revive him, and it wasn't grief that made her eyes glisten, nor sent the tears coursing down her cheeks. Even while she wept so silently, there was a smile upon her lips, a small, sweet, tender thing. It was plain that she was unaware of Wentworth in the doorway. A sob shook her and she bent over James, crushed her mouth to his. She eased his head to the floor, jumped to her feet and flung a wild look about the room. It was then she saw Wentworth. Blood flushed into her throat and cheeks, but she laughed and struck an attitude, folding her arms and pretending to twist a non-existent mustache.

"The proud beauty was in my power!" She grinned and dropped her pose. "Honest, he was so handsome lying there, I just had to take advantage of his hapless innocence."

Wentworth was frankly puzzled. A few moments ago, she had helped a killer she was supposed to love to escape from the law, and now she wept over the unconscious form of the detective. Yet there seemed no doubt about her love for Charlton....

Wentworth shrugged his shoulders over the problem, ordered

her curtly aside and bent over James, nodded. Judging from the pulse and the eye reaction, James would be coming out of it without help in about five minutes. He snatched a piece of paper from his pocket, scribbled on it rapidly and fastened it about the throat of Paul Collins. Then he heaved the unconscious racketeer to his shoulder, motioned to Margie and wrapped his fingers about her arm. She went with him with a lassitude that she tried to hide, and Wentworth entered Collins' waiting limousine and left the neighborhood. A half dozen blocks away, he changed to a taxi, leaving Collins, but taking the girl. Margie still tried to make a jest of the whole affair. She murmured a song....

"You wouldn't dare insult me, if my brother, Jack, were here...."

Wentworth leaned into his corner of the seat and studied the girl's pert face in the transient light of the street lamps. Somewhere in her complex emotions lay the solution of all his difficulties, he knew. If he could use her properly, he could find Charlton and LeFevre, force them to reveal the power behind them. Margie moved restlessly under his scrutiny.

"You aren't taking me to the cops," she conjectured, "or you'd have left me with the old Bandit back there. So what's up?"

Wentworth's lips were stiff in their smiling. This girl was torn in her loyalties, but she suffered no such pain as he. Her lover was not in the grip of an insanity that racked its victim in endless homicidal rages. His lips twitched....

"At my home," he said quietly, "I have some food which has been impregnated with the insanity drug that Charlton, among others, is dispensing."

"Oh, he isn't!" Margie cried. "Honest, he isn't! He's only helping the man…" She broke off, shook her head. "Charlie wouldn't do a thing like that."

Wentworth still spoke quietly. "That note which I fastened about Collins' neck was directed to Charlton. I told him that if he didn't come to my apartment for you within twenty-four hours that…" He paused and Margie pulled forward to the edge of her seat, sat there very rigidly. She laughed wildly, choked back the sound. Wentworth concluded, "that I would feed you some of that drugged food."

MARGIE SAT very still, twisting her hands in her lap. The taxi drew to the curb and she moved woodenly after Wentworth, walked beside him into his apartment house. The rouge appeared spotted on her pale cheeks. She flung out her hands in a wide, pleading gesture.

"It won't do any good," she cried. "It won't!"

Wentworth gestured silently for her to enter the elevator ahead of him, was gravely courteous as he ushered her into his home. The nurses in attendance upon Nita had set the place a little to rights, but for Wentworth, it held an empty, unattended air. His lips closed a little more firmly. His face had a gaunt, stretched look.

"I wanted you to see my fiancée," he said.

Margie Huron lifted her head, shook herself a little and managed a smile. "Okay. If I'm going nuts, I'm going nuts, but you needn't wait the twenty-four hours. Charlie won't come. I met Miss van Sloan here before, didn't I? I'll enjoy a chat."

Wentworth's lips twitched. He shut his fists hard. "There won't be any chat," he said woodenly, gestured her toward the door to the hall. Her eyes widened a little, but she obeyed. A nurse in stiffly starched uniform met them at the entrance to Nita's room.

"The doctor is with her," she said quietly. "You may go in."

"I didn't know she was sick," Margie said quickly. "I'm sorry."

Wentworth smiled curiously, pushed open the door. Margie went forward slowly. A scream rose to her throat and she bit hard on her hand to stop the cry. Beside the bed, Dr. Higgens turned angrily. His eyes held cold glittering points as they swung to Wentworth, but his indignation faded quickly. Wentworth put a hand on Margie's shoulder and thrust her roughly forward, then he turned and stared down at the bed. Bonds still held Nita motionless. It was apparent that she was under the influence of opiates, but even so, her head tossed in the impotence of her ceaseless rage and there was a wild, staring look in her eyes. Her mouth twisted hideously, senselessly. Wentworth forced himself to gaze while anger and pain tore at him like searing pincers. Margie was sobbing wildly, trying to strangle the sounds.

"Is there anything new, Doctor?" Wentworth asked, hearing his voice, strange and hoarse, crack loudly through the room.

"Nothing," Higgins answered quietly. "I had hoped that if the derangement was caused by drugs it would wear off, but there seems to be no abatement."

The room blurred before Wentworth's eyes. He took tight hold of himself and spoke very carefully. "And your experiments?"

"Nothing yet."

Wentworth turned and stumbled from the room. But this

97

couldn't last. It couldn't. Nita wasn't lost to him. In the other cases, the insanity had cleared up after a while. Nita had simply received a larger dosage, that was all. Her recovery would be slower… Wentworth told himself those things deliberately and fought down the thoughts that pointed ghostly fingers at him, that mocked him from the dark corners of the hallway through which he stumbled. The drugs that Nita had taken were intended for the Spider. LeFevre would not be content with a temporary madness for the Spider. He would want him to howl his insanity through the years….

WENTWORTH FOUGHT himself to calmness, feeling Margie Huron's hand upon his arm. "I didn't know. I didn't know!" she gabbled. "Honest, I didn't know. I've been trying to make Charlie stop, but he says he can't. I don't think he wants to, but he wouldn't do a thing like this. I've known his every thought for so long… He's a wild boy, that's all… Oh, why do you look at me like that? I didn't have anything to do with it. You know I didn't!"

Margie turned, flung herself down on a davenport and buried her face in her hands. Wentworth walked over and stood staring down at her with burning eyes.

"In twenty-four hours," he said heavily, "if Charlton doesn't come, you will eat the same food Nita ate."

He took the girl then and locked her in a room whose only window opened on fifteen stories of empty space. He had to whip himself into action. There were tasks to be done. He had a definite plan of action ahead, but the sight of Nita had unnerved him. He phoned Kirkpatrick and the Commissioner's voice was dull with fatigue.

"I had Hanson on the carpet and he just about convinced me of his innocence," he said. "A half hour later, he went crazy and jumped out of a window. He seemed to be under the influence of the drug, too. No, I don't think it was part of a plot. Just general terrorism…."

Wentworth frowned, shook his head over the news and asked about Detective James.

"Something about him has changed," Kirkpatrick said. "He has never been hard. An efficient investigator, but not the type I would assign to a dangerous arrest, or to clean out a criminal hang-out, although he is an excellent marksman…" It was plain that Kirkpatrick's mind was not on what he said. He broke off abruptly. "Dick, there have been fifteen cases of violent insanity tonight in addition to Hanson, and more than a hundred casualties as a result. It doesn't seem to me that LeFevre is confining himself any longer to victims who can pay.

"Only one man has reported threats to police during the last twenty-four hours. I think LeFevre has them pretty well cowed with his recurrent insanity. Dick, we've got to do something at once."

Wentworth laughed shortly. Do something, yes, but what? He had his plan… "I'm going to call in newspaper men in the morning," he said heavily, "through them I'm going to challenge LeFevre. I hurt him in two or three ways today, breaking up hiding places of his men and killing a few. He may be angry enough to accept the challenge "

Kirkpatrick's voice suddenly came to life, "Preposterous, Dick! You don't think for a moment that he would play fair if he did accept your challenge!"

Wentworth smiled into the transmitter. "No," he agreed quietly.

"Dick, then it's madness!"

Wentworth laughed wildly, "There seems to be a lot of it going around! Kirk, I want your promise not to interfere. I suspect that you had Jesse James following me today. At any rate, some one saved my life today and James showed up afterward on my trail. There must be no interference!"

Kirkpatrick was silent for a long time. "I can't promise, Dick," he said finally. "If you were killed… How is Nita, Dick? Is there any change."

"None," Wentworth said dully. "Good night, Kirk." He hung up and walked with dragging feet through the drawing-room to the terrace. The dawn wind was fresh and off to the East there was a tinge of rose on the clouds. Wentworth turned his back on it and went to his bed, dropped on his side. His face twisted in abrupt, hard anger. He thought: *Nita…!*

CHAPTER 7
"SABRES—TO THE DEATH!"

WENTWORTH ALLOWED himself only a few hours of sleep, whipped the lethargy from his brain and body with a cold shower. He fed himself and his prisoner, then summoned newspaper men to his apartment, and through them

The insane policemen were hacking fiercely at the wire!

issued his challenge to LeFevre. He pledged that police should not be given any information at all, stated his willingness to meet LeFevre, "any time, any place, with any weapon...."

Throughout the day, waiting for LeFevre to communicate, he remained in his penthouse. Restless energy kept him prowling about the terrace. Twice, at Higgins' request, he took his violin to Nita's room and tried to soothe her with music. Newspaper men and men from Kirkpatrick called at frequent intervals, but he refused them any information. He kept away from Margie Huron. When another dawn came, he would go to her with the drugged food....

At mid-afternoon, Kirkpatrick called again. "Not trying to worm anything out of you," he said curtly. "I want your advice. LeFevre has demanded certain chemical secrets from Professor Rolab, with the usual threat. This time, he declares he will destroy Rolab's mind permanently. Rolab is scheduled to make an address before the American Scientific Union this afternoon, and he wants protection. On my instruction, he has been fasting all day. Even when we are reasonably sure his food is pure, we thought it best to take that precaution. I wondered if you would go to the meeting with me? In about a half hour?"

Wentworth deliberated a moment, then shook his head. "Not unless I have heard from LeFevre in the meantime," he said.

"He won't communicate with you," Kirkpatrick barked impatiently. "If he did, I wouldn't permit you to fight the duel!"

Wentworth laughed softly, but made no other reply and Kirkpatrick hung up explosively. Five minutes had not elapsed when the instrument rang again and a voice that Wentworth recognized came tauntingly over the wire.

"Your challenge is accepted, *m'sieur*," LeFevre said mockingly. "My associates tell me I am *fou*—what you call crazy—to do it. They say I have taken of my own drug. Nevertheless...."

"Come to the point," Wentworth said shortly, "I don't like you well enough to enjoy your conversation." His heart was thumping high and hard in this breast, with a suffocating joy. He had stirred hatred in LeFevre's breast, had piqued him to the point of a duel! "When, where, and what weapon?" he demanded.

"I will call you just after dawn tomorrow and give the place," LeFevre said lightly. "I accept your word that there will be none of *les flicks,* the police...."

Wentworth informed LeFevre briefly, controlling his voice with an effort, that he was threatened with surveillance and that it probably would be better if he could elude the police and phone LeFevre somewhere at an appointed hour, but the Frenchman laughed.

"I can trus' you to avoid *les flicks* after I call, *m'sieur*," he said. "I am sorry for the informality of these arrangements, but your friend, I do not know, and you ask that I call... Ah, yes, *m'sieur*, the weapon! It shall be the *rapier*. I have a fine pair, the mos' excellent, but bring yours if you prefer."

Wentworth quietly replaced the phone, stared directly before him through long minutes. He was under no delusions as to LeFevre's good faith. It might well be that he would use the rendezvous solely to kill Wentworth. That was a chance which had to be taken. Wentworth was determined that if he laid eyes again on LeFevre, the Frenchman should die. It was plain that he was the key man of the conspiracy. If he were destroyed, the man behind him would be forced out into the open... Despite the long odds against success and the personal peril involved, Wentworth began to feel an odd exuberance. He sprang to his feet and strode energetically about his apartment. Higgins came wearily from the laboratory he had rigged in a spare guest room to watch him.

"I'm beginning to think there weren't any drugs," he said impatiently. He brushed his wiry, red hair flat to his scalp with a jerky hand and it sprang straight up again. "Tried every damned thing...."

"Brownlee precipitation test?" Wentworth flung at him. "Remember what the old professor found out about certain compounds of strychnine?"

HIGGINS STARED at Wentworth with eyes gone owlish, whipped about and strode back into his laboratory. He made a great clatter of glass, popped back to the door.

"Why in the hell didn't you say so hours ago?" he demanded, and vanished again before Wentworth could answer. Wentworth tipped back his head and laughed. After so long a despair, he knew hope. He made rapid preparations for leaving the apartment. He would have Kirkpatrick set a police guard over Margie while he sought to help protect the threatened scientists....

Within a half hour, he was on his way to the rendezvous with Kirkpatrick. His mind was intent on plans for triumph over LeFevre. He was confident of his own ability with the sabre, but he knew that victory or defeat would not be determined in the duel itself. The Frenchman would plan treachery to kill him there. When the duel failed, he would spring his real trap. And Wentworth must go into this alone. There was no doubt in his mind that if he allowed himself to be followed, LeFevre would surely discover it and simply fail to meet him. So the Spider would go alone into almost certain death for the slim gamble which might give him a decisive victory.

Wentworth made arrangements to meet Kirkpatrick at Winthrop Hall where the scientists were holding their speaking program. The Hall was near the new Medical Center on the East Side and Wentworth took a taxi, settled back on the cushions to relax, turned on the radio. A news broadcaster was speaking:

"Police believe that the insanity is caused by drugs and that these drugs are given to intended victims in their food or drink. Apparently, cooking has no effect at all on the drugs, and doctors cannot yet discover the drug or tell how to destroy it. Therefore, all the people are warned…."

Wentworth switched off the radio, and the taxi driver shifted uneasily in his seat. "Geez, am I glad I ain't got money!" he shouted. "It's a case of them that has gitting it in the neck."

Abruptly, Wentworth whipped forward in his seat. "Look out, man!" he cried. The brakes took hold with a squeal, but when the driver saw where Wentworth pointed, he kicked the accelerator to the floor. Four men were charging them—four men who ran with the slouching, feral mien of beasts. One held a gun in his fist, the others held knives and clubs. They started out to block the taxi and in so doing one of them bumped against another. Instantly, the four were embroiled in a snarling, mad quarrel, slashing at one another without discrimination. "Slow down!" Wentworth insisted.

"Not me, mister," the driver yelled. "You may want to get yourself killed, but...."

Wentworth prodded the man's neck with an automatic and, with a terrified glance over his shoulder, the man jerked to a stop. "Geez, mister, you ain't gone nuts, too, have you?"

Wentworth ignored him, peering back toward the spot where the four madmen had been fighting. Only one remained on his feet, and he was slashing, slashing with his knife at men who were plainly already quite dead. Even as he watched, a strange and horrible thing began to happen. Out of doors and windows, mad faces appeared. A woman with a long iron poker in her hands crept on the madman in the street. At a window, two women tore at each other with a fierceness that could mean only mania. With a shock that almost stunned him, Wentworth realized that practically everyone in this entire section of the city had been drugged; that raving, murderous insanity gripped them all!

"For God's sake, mister!" the taxi driver pleaded.

""Police house around the corner," Wentworth hurled at him. "Get to it fast! Tell them the whole precinct has gone crazy. Tell them Richard Wentworth sent you." He jumped to the street and the taxi surged away. But what could he do against these countless mad men and women? Short of knocking them unconscious, or killing them, he could not stop their homicidal activities. He was very likely to be overwhelmed and slain himself. But, good God, there must be a few sane persons amid all this horror. He must find and lead them to safety, to the police house....

HE RAN toward the sidewalk, evaded the heavy iron poker which the woman swung at him and jabbed at nerve centers in her throat. She spilled, unconscious, to the pavement, and Wentworth ducked into a nearby doorway. Instantly, he was fighting for his life against two crazed men who had lurked there, awaiting a victim. Fortunately, they had no weapons and he succeeded in dropping them, too. His hat was gone, his coat ripped from his shoulders and there were bloody scratches across his face. He stood there in the dimness of the hall panting, searching the shadows for others who might threaten his safety, then raced up the stairs. He must open all doors, try to discover if any sane persons still remained to be saved. Twice he narrowly escaped being killed, but finally he had gathered a dozen persons, all women save two, who in some unknown way had not been stricken. He ran ahead of them down the stairs to clear the way for their escape.

"Around the corner to the police house," he told them. "They already know what's happening. They'll take care of you."

He ran ahead and behind him a woman screamed with frantic hoarseness of terror. Unseen in the shadows, a man had hidden, to spring on her when the others had passed. Panic stampeded the others and Wentworth fought vainly to break through the stream to the rescue. He was battered by clawing fists, tripped and kicked, but finally the women were past him and he could run back. He was too late. A gloating madman had strangled a girl to death horribly.

There was nothing to be done. Execution of the madman would accomplish nothing. Tomorrow, he might regain his senses and know nothing of this horror. Wentworth knocked him to the floor, left him lying beside the woman he had slain. At least, the man would do no more killing for a while. Choked with the horror of the madness that was all about him, Wentworth ran on to captain the fleeing women again. He found them in the first floor hall where one of them, an Italian girl, had managed to rally them. Her black hair was streaming about her shoulders, which, strangely, were bare. He saw that she wore an evening gown of bright scarlet.

The girl smiled at him with a frightened flash of white teeth. "My dress?" she laughed "I was having it fitted. And now mama... mama..." Horror twisted her face. "Oh, *signor,* she throw herself out of the window...!"

Wentworth shook her. "Snap out of it. I need your help," he ordered her briskly. "Help me take these women to the police house..." The girl fought against the shudders that shook her.

"*Sí, sí,*" she whispered. "I... help."

Out into the street, Wentworth led his small group. The air was filled with the screamings and mouthing of mad people. In the middle of the pavement, a man was stripping clothing from a woman viciously. She made no effort to escape. She was intent only on sinking her teeth into his throat. Blood ran from her mouth corners... At a pelting run, Wentworth led the fugitives away. Around the corner, up the steps of the police house and into the sanctuary of the great hall behind the heavy doors. They clapped shut heavily behind the little band and Wentworth stood rigidly, staring down at what lay upon the floor. It was the taxi driver. He lay belly-down, but his head had been twisted so that his face grinned terribly up at the ceiling. Off, somewhere in the building, a man screamed sobbingly, once, twice, began a third time… and stopped. The silence ached with the suddenness of that scream's end.

"Up the steps," Wentworth ordered sharply. "Up the steps. I can defend you there…."

Huddled together, the fugitives crept toward the steps. From the high doorway opening to the right, a man in police uniform sprang. It was the girl in red he seized. Wentworth was on him instantly. A single, sweeping swing on his automatic smashed the cop to the floor. The girl clung to Wentworth, saying nothing, not even crying, but her breath came in long, quavering sobs. "Up the steps!" Wentworth screamed again.

FROM THE darkness of the hall, a gun blazed and Wentworth's automatic bucked in his hand. The thump of the gunman's body, falling, made the building quiver. The fugitives were all on the stairs. He brought up the rear, thrusting the girl ahead of him. They were no more than half-way up the first flight when the hall was filled with a mob of fighting, shouting madmen. They were in police blue, but that made the terror greater, and they all had guns….

Women screamed their frantic way up the steps. Wentworth hurled himself flat on the floor at their head and—held his guns ready. God knew be did not want to fire on these men who tomorrow might be as ready to defend these people as he was now, but if they came shooting… Crazily, the police rushed the stairs, some firing as they came. A woman gasped with pain and pitched to the floor not a yard from Wentworth. With a curse, he opened fire. He had no choice. Fear would not stop these men. Nothing less than bullets would do. He picked three men in the lead and shot each of them through the thigh. Their backward fall swept the whole charging horde down the steps again—where their companions butchered them like hogs. Blackjacks and clubbed pistols smashed their skulls. Guns, at point blank range, blew them open.

"The stairway to the roof!" Wentworth knew it was the brave little Italian girl whispering into his ear. "It has a door. It can lock."

"Get them up there," Wentworth ordered swiftly. "I'll hold them off till you're ready."

Already, the madmen were reforming for the attack. Wentworth glanced behind him. He must have some additional cover, at least some point to which he could retreat should they succeed in storming the stairs. With an eager shout, he sprang to his feet. The fire hose! He sprang at the valve wheel, whirled it wide open before he grabbed the hose and the pressure of the water whirled it on its reel. He snatched the nozzle, stood ready to defend the head of the steps. The men were almost upon him when the powerful stream of water pounded into their faces. Wentworth was forced to shoot two of the men who fought against him, but the others were washed off their feet.

With swift hands then, he wedged the hose between the

palings of the railing so that it swept at an angle across the entire width of the steps. Then he sprang away down the hall. The last of the women had climbed the stairs and the Italian girl was waiting. He thrust her inside, swung the door shut and locked it, urged his small band to the roof. When he turned that fire hose valve, he knew that he had sounded a fire-alarm. Probably police reserves would come too, since the alarm was from a police station. If he could hold on for a short while longer....

The afternoon sun blazed down hotly on the roof and the women crouched in the shadow of the kiosk which housed the stair-head. But if Wentworth had thought to find sanctuary for his flock here, he had taken no account of the other roofs which were separated from this one only by high, spiked iron fences. Already slobbering men were swarming over these and their screams were summoning dozens more out of roof scuttles along the entire line of tenements. And the mad police already were hacking persistently at the door below. Wentworth flung a frantic look about him. The radio aerial!

Stretching the whole length of the police station building, it was comprised of five strands of powerful copper wire.

Swiftly, he shouted instructions and the women, frightened into forgetting their panic, leaped to obey under the leadership of the girl in red. The aerial was snatched from its standards and twisted, by means of its stretchers, into a tight rope. Wentworth, watching the work, threw three swift shots through the door below, dropped two men who had succeeded in mounting the iron fence, and ran to the help of the women. The wire rope already dangled over the roof's edge. A stretcher had been hooked into a vent pipe, but women shrank from the danger of that long drop to the earth behind the police station. There was no time to make slings and lower them, one by one, so Wentworth drove them to the rope. His face was cut by harsh lines. If one of the women should release her hold for so much as a second....

Forcing them to wrap the five-stranded wire about legs and arms, he drove them over. When two women had made the trip safely, the others did not resist so much. Twice more Wentworth had to shoot down madmen who thronged to the fence and suddenly, the stair kiosk vomited forth a line of maniac police. Wentworth flung himself prone outside the parapet which circled the roof and began shooting. It was a matter of moments only, he knew. On such a wide front as the police advanced, it would be impossible for one man to hold them back. He emptied his automatics in swift succession and felt the girl's hand on his shoulder.

"It's all right now," she whispered. "They're all gone...."

Wentworth glanced toward her and saw that she was standing, with no effort to take advantage of the parapet's protection. Even as he reached to snatch her to cover, she reeled, half-lifted her hands to her head and slumped forward across Wentworth's body. With a curse, he seized the girl and jumped to the wires. Would it hold them both? He had no way of telling, but he must take the chance. He stopped long enough to reload one automatic, to throw a few shots to stop the charge of the madmen, then he took the unconscious girl over his shoulder and swung out into space. The wires burned into his palm and instantly, the police were at the edge above him, hacking at the wires which alone held them from the fatal plunge to the earth. Already, a new peril loomed below. From a window directly in their path, knives and hands reached out eagerly to slaughter them.

Grimly, Wentworth shut his lips. If he abandoned the girl, he might be able to fight his way through, for in that way, he could bring both guns to bear on the mad killers who stormed them from every side. But that meant letting the brave girl fall to her death. True, she was wounded. There had been no time to determine how badly. She might already be dead... Something like laughter beat at Wentworth's teeth. Even if she were dead, he would not drop her, he knew. It could not hurt her corpse, that fall, but she had fought loyally at his side. When she might have climbed down to safety, she had delayed to tell him that the way was clear for his own escape....

Wentworth twisted about on his wire rope and shot twice at the men who sought to hack the strands. A body, hurtling downward, almost brushed him from his precarious hold. For the moment, they were safe from that angle, but the window below...! A gun blasted from it and Wentworth felt the warm fan of the lead. Only the fact that the madmen were crowding frantically into that narrow space, each one anxious to kill, prevented any single one of them from taking accurate aim. Three shots were left in the automatic. There would be no more chance to reload before he reached the ground, still many feet away.

He brought his gun to bear on the men in the window and, at that moment, felt the girl stir in his arms. She lifted her head and stared into Wentworth's face. For a moment her eyes were blank and then, suddenly, terribly, they changed. She reached out her clawing hands and tore at Wentworth's eyes. She writhed and fought against his grip. *She was insane!*

Wentworth felt a jar in the wire that he gripped and knew that the madmen were at work again on the edge of the roof, that they had succeeded in snapping one of the few feeble strands that held him from death. A gun blasted again from the window and Wentworth felt it pluck at his shirt at the same moment the girl succeeded in fastening her teeth deeply in his arm—the arm which, wrapped about the wire, alone held them from plunging to death in the paved courtyard, thirty feet below!

CHAPTER 8
PENDULUM OF DEATH

DEATH HOVERED very close to Wentworth as he dangled on the weakening wires. No one could possibly help him now. Somehow, he must fight his own way clear, and it must be quickly! He released his hold on the girl for the moment, allowing her to cling with her own strength. Mad as she was, she recognized the peril of the empty space beneath her. She ceased to attack Wentworth and gripped him desperately with both arms. His gun arm freed, he bullet-swept the window where madmen extended guns and knives, then he dropped swiftly toward the earth. The wires seemed red hot as they ripped across his flesh, but he dared not slow his descent. There were no bullets left to hurl at those men who hacked at the wires. The cutting of one more strand might hurl him, spinning, to his death....

Wentworth was still ten feet above the earth when the wires snapped and, hampered by the girl as he was, he had difficulty in maintaining his balance. Striking the ground, he lay for a moment stunned, but, even so, he drove himself to his feet. The girl was unconscious, a crumpled, pitiful thing in her torn dress of red. The other women huddled about him, seeking succor, but this part of the battle was over. Sirens moaned swiftly nearer. Wentworth led his charges by a roundabout way to the streets... A taxi driver demurred on taking him as a passenger until he had shown sufficient money for the fare and, for the first time, Wentworth realized the picture he must present. His shirt was torn and bloody, his coat gone, his face scratched. He must seem a madman himself. Swiftly he changed his directions and went to his home for fresh clothing before he once more sped to Winthrop Hall and Commissioner Kirkpatrick. The meeting would be almost over... Police guards were at the doors of the Hall and they directed Wentworth to the main floor.

"Commissioner's orders, sir," they told him. "Don't want folks to know he's here."

There were two hundred men in the auditorium, all of them distinguished scientists. Newspaper men were sprawled at a table near the platform on which a short, earnest man who wore a scraggly beard was talking with energetic gestures. Wentworth recognized him instantly as the man Kirkpatrick had said was threatened, Professor Rolab. As he listened to the man's heavily accented speech, Wentworth felt a tenseness spread over his entire body. This man, of whom LeFevre had demanded his secrets, had discovered a cure for the bubonic plague, the dread Black Death which had slaughtered millions through the ages. God, what a weapon that disease would be in criminal hands! A man who had dared to release wholesale insanity on the world would not hesitate to loose this greater slaughter. That done, his cure would be sold for countless millions....

Wentworth's attention snapped back to the stage. There was a curious thickening of Professor Rolab's voice, a certain erratic jerkiness about his gestures. Once he stopped for several seconds in his address and pressed his hand to his head, then he went hurriedly on. He held a test-tube high above his head.

"In this tube," he said thickly, "there are enough bubonic germs to wipe out the entire city of New York. I intend to demonstrate my cure here. A microscope, a few drops of my 'phage and you will see the germs die." He stood motionless, holding the tube above his head. "See the germs die!" he shrieked.

With an oath, Wentworth sprinted down the aisle. He knew abruptly why the man was hesitant and erratic in speech and movements. The drugs of insanity were working on his brain!

"Get that tube away from him!" Wentworth shouted. "He's insane. Get that tube...!"

GOOD GOD! If that tube were hurled among the scientists gathered here, they would be terribly stricken. There could be no doubt that many of them would fall victim to the fearful Black Death. It might well be impossible to confine the germs to the hall....

"*Get that tube!*" Wentworth shouted.

Even as he cried the words aloud, he realized that no one could reach Professor Rolab in time. The scientist had drawn back his arm to hurl the tube out over the audience. Even a shot would only smash the tube when Rolab fell....

Wentworth saw that Kirkpatrick was closer to the platform than himself, that he recognized the danger and was making a frantic charge to reach Rolab before it was too late.

Rolab began to laugh stridently. "Fools! Charlatans!" he cried. "You doubt my cure? Ha, I will give you a test! You shall all have the Black Death! And I shall cure you!" He laughed again, jerked back his arm and hurled the tube far out over the crowd.

Panic seized the audience. They had been rigid, without realization of what threatened. Now, terribly, they knew, and the knowledge rocked them like an explosion. Men leaped to their feet everywhere and fought to get out of the path of that hurtling tube, battled to reach the exit doors. One man alone tried to breast that stream. Springing to the seats, jumping from one to another, Wentworth fought to get under the tube, to snatch it in the air. If he seized it very carefully and could hold his balance afterward...!

A shout rose in his throat as he realized that the glittering vial of death would pass over his head. There was no chance that it would not break. Frantically, Wentworth hurled himself into the air. His fingertips brushed the test tube, broke its flight. Falling across the seats, Wentworth paid no heed at all to what lay beneath him. His fingers touched it again. *He had it!* But even as he grasped it, his knee caught the back of the seats over which he had jumped precariously and in a gigantic clatter of falling

117

chairs, a splintering of wood, Wentworth crashed to the floor. With no thought of personal injury, he held the vial high over his head. A chair back thudded against the back of his skull and half dazed him. His back thumped violently to the floor and a panic stricken man stepped on his chest, brushing the arm that held the test tube. Wentworth knew a moment of total blackness, of excruciating pain, then his senses and vision rushed back to him. He still held the test tube rigidly above his head.

Shuddering, he struggled to his feet. The doors were jammed with fleeing men. On the stage, Kirkpatrick had closed with Rolab and police reserves were crashing in from all sides. Wentworth made his cautious way to the platform and laid the tube of deadly germs in their cotton-wood casing. His breath came in shuddering gasps and, when he had put the thing down, he collapsed into a chair, twitching with the universal shudder of his nerves. He was aware presently of Kirkpatrick standing over him, of his friend's hand, warm on his shoulder. He got to his feet, forced a grin to his lips.

"That was a close thing in there," he said quietly.

"No other man on earth," Kirkpatrick said vehemently, "would have done what you did. Dick, for God's sake, don't go to duel LeFevre. You wouldn't be here if he hadn't accepted your challenge. We… we can't spare you, old man!"

Wentworth put a cautious hand to his back, winced. "If I don't get some arnica on this back," he said, "you needn't worry about my meeting LeFevre. I won't be able to move."

Kirkpatrick accepted his defeat with a shrug. "I know you've promised him that police won't follow you, but, damn it, Dick, you're not going to duel LeFevre if I have to put you in jail! You know that he has no intention of fighting fairly."

WENTWORTH STARED very directly into Kirkpatrick's eyes. "Don't press me too far, Kirk," he said quietly. "Don't you realize how important it is that we find LeFevre? All our efforts so far haven't come within a mile of him. He continues at large and he continues to drive men insane while police and every other facility of the country protect him. Damn it, Kirk, we've got to get LeFevre or there won't be a sane person left in the city!"

"It won't do you any good to get killed by LeFevre," Kirkpatrick insisted stubbornly.

Wentworth gripped his arm. "I have no intention of being killed, nor of being tricked by LeFevre. Will you believe me?"

Kirkpatrick's stiff lips twitched. "I have to, Dick," he replied hoarsely. "I have to. I don't want you to go and yet I know what you say is true. You're our only hope. But, damn it, Dick, I'm going to have men on your trail! They'll be ready all over the city and if we see LeFevre or anything that looks like a duel...."

Wentworth laughed. "That's swell. We'll do that." He went heavily home. It was twelve hours before he could hope to hear from LeFevre, and by that time, God alone knew what could happen to the people. It was apparent that he had changed his plans of attack and was no longer satisfied with the money he could mulct from the wealthy by extortion. Wentworth could not understand the purpose behind the wholesale attack upon the people of the East Side upon which he had stumbled, but he could not doubt that LeFevre expected to profit from it in some way… Such schemes as that were under way, and Wentworth could only wait the fruition of his plans.

Wentworth was incapable of resting that night. He slept sporadically, and often he was in the laboratory at work with Higgins on his experiments. Higgins' face had a gray, weary cast, but he would not cease his tests. Wentworth knew that there was need for urgency, but it seemed to him that Higgins had labored past endurance, past the ability to think clearly.

"Why not rest a few hours?" Wentworth urged. "The antidote for the insanity drug will be just as effective then. And your brain will be clearer…."

Higgins whirled about furiously. "Talk about something you know!" he shouted. "Go and fight your battles. Leave me alone!"

Wentworth stared at him with a hard suspicion now stirring in his brain. Good God! Surely Higgins had not taken of the drug, too?

As he watched him, Higgins relaxed, shook his head with a crooked smile on his lips.

"Forgive me, Dick," he begged quietly. "I'm pretty well tuckered. The truth is, Dick, that unless we can perfect this drug before about noon tomorrow…."

Wentworth gripped his arm with sudden urgency, feeling fear tug at his heart with cold fingers.

"It's quite clear," Higgins went on woodenly, "that Nita received an extra heavy dosage of the stuff. It is my belief that the drug is still working on her brain, growing in strength all the time, and that unless we can interrupt that…."

Wentworth released his hold on Higgins' arm, reeled backward a step. Then he braced himself and stood very rigidly facing the doctor.

"You're saying that unless you can work out the antidote that Nita...?"

Higgins nodded, "She will be... permanently insane."

WENTWORTH STOOD very still, staring unseeingly into the doctor's harsh lined face. He whispered, "Permanently... insane!" They were just words with out meaning. He cursed terribly and a light-headedness blunted his senses. He realized that Higgins was pressing a glass to his lips.

"Drink, you damned fool!" Higgins growled. "Then get out of here and let me work."

Wentworth gulped the stuff and felt it take fiery hold of his heart. He drew in a deep breath "All right, Higgins. If there's anything I can do...?"

"Get out," Higgins snapped again. He was already back at the bench he had rigged against one wall of the room, bending over the bubbling of a small retort. Wentworth went heavily from the laboratory. Before noon. Eight more hours. Eight hours was a lot of time, a lot of time. In an hour, it would be dawn and LeFevre would phone him an appointment for a duel. Wentworth found himself in the drawing-room and sat down very carefully, as if his body were fragile. Eight hours. He got up again and walked along the hall. Nita was sleeping, a drugged sleep, the nurse said. Her eyes were full of commiseration.

"Why pity me?" Wentworth demanded harshly. "It's because she saved me that she's this way!"

"You mustn't think things like that," the nurse retorted speaking with a hurried softness "You mustn't say things like that!"

Wentworth strode blindly past her. In an hour, he was going out to meet LeFevre, the man who had done this to Nita. LeFevre would not meet him fairly. He would try to kill him by foul means. If Wentworth permitted the police to follow, LeFevre simply would not meet him.

"This won't do," Wentworth mused heavily, aloud. "This won't do. You've got to get hold of yourself." He had to make plans, so that if he failed with LeFevre, he still would have a way to win.

He went to the kitchen and got together a breakfast, took it to Margie Huron's room. The police guard still stood stolidly before it.

"You're dismissed," Wentworth told him. "I'll handle this from now on."

The officer saluted gratefully, yawned as he went off down the hall. He'd go home to sleep now. Wentworth thought, watching him. Home… He unlocked the door quietly. Margie was stretched out across the bed, her head of long red hair dangling over the edge. For a moment, he thought that she was dead, then he saw her breasts move with her breathing and saw that she had simply fallen into an exhausted sleep. He set the breakfast tray on a table beside the bed, locked the door and turned on the ceiling light.

"Margie!" he said quietly. "The twenty four hours are up!"

The girl jerked to a sitting position, eyes staring wildly. She remained rigid for a moment, then she slumped back on the bed and gave Wentworth a pale grin.

"I told you Charlie wouldn't come," she said. "Little Margie must be quite some judge of character."

Wentworth motioned toward the food. "Why cling to him then? Why take this way out?"

Margie shook her red head, smiling slightly. "Now, is that nice, Mr. Wentworth? Asking me to turn rat that way?"

Wentworth shrugged, his eyes burning into hers. "I was told a few moments ago that if some antidote isn't found before noon Nita will be… permanently insane. Charlton is responsible for that, and you defend him."

Margie shook her head. She leaned forward. "I don't defend him. I don't do that. It's a horrible thing, but, can't you see, I love him. It doesn't matter that he didn't come to help me. Nothing matters except that—oh, hell! I'm talking like a sob story. Give me the grub."

She reached for the tray, "You cook this? Quite some cook, you are. And I love cheese omelets."

Wentworth said, slowly, "It was a piece of cheese that contained the drug which drove Nita insane."

MARGIE'S FACE was very pale. She couldn't look at the food. Her eyes clung to Wentworth's. "You know, I've opened that window over there at least twenty-five times during the night. I think if it hadn't been quite so far to the ground…" She shuddered, matched up a fork and carried a fragment of the omelet to her lips. Wentworth's eyes stayed implacably on her face.

"You could avoid that if you wished," he said quietly. "I only want to know where to find Charlton or LeFevre."

Margie's eyes had a fixed, glazed look. She opened her lips and seemed actually to force her hand to deposit the food in her mouth. She swallowed convulsively and leaned back against the headboard, panting heavily.

"There, by God," she whispered. "I have got guts. I'd bet Socrates didn't take the hemlock any better than I did that egg." A little shudder shook her. "How long will it be?"

Wentworth did not answer, only stood looking at her. Margie jumped to her feet, caught hold of Wentworth's arm.

"How long will it be?" she demanded, forcing the words out harshly.

"You must love him a great deal," he said very quietly. "It will be a long time, Margie."

Margie's eyes, gazing up at Wentworth's, began to widen very slowly. She clung to his arms, "What are you saying?" she whispered. "What are you saying?"

Wentworth shook his head slowly. "Did you really think I'd give you the drug, Margie?" he asked heavily. "So far as I know, that food was quite pure."

Margie fainted and Wentworth eased her across the bed, crossed to the window and stood looking out toward the sky that was showing the first gray hint of dawn. He wasn't thinking.

He was past thought. He felt that LeFevre would phone soon… He started when Margie's hand touched his arm, turned slowly.

"You wanted to break me, is that it?" she whispered.

Wentworth laughed shortly, "I intended to give you the drug," he said. "I found I couldn't. Now get the hell out of here. If you

124

see Charlton again, tell him I'll kill him on sight. Get out, I tell you!" He was shouting. This girl was sane, this lover of a crook was sane, and Nita, loyal and fine... He shook his fists over his head. *"Get out!"*

Margie stood on tiptoes and threw her arms around his neck. Her kiss clung to his lips and the danger and the fury went out of Wentworth in a breath. He took Margie's shoulders in his hands.

"You're too fine to be in with those crooks," he said more quietly. "You'll find that out some day. You're free to go...."

The distant buzzing of the telephone electrified Wentworth. He went striding to answer it. LeFevre's voice was cool and mocking.

"Leave the house within a minute, Wentworth," he said, "and do not use your phone again for any purpose in the meantime—otherwise I shall not meet you. Drive straight up Fifth Avenue. When we are sure that you aren't followed, we'll make contact. We shall fight on a roof, my enemy. *Au 'voir...!"*

Wentworth bounded along the hall. His languor and his heaviness were gone. In his brain was only one thought, to cause the death of LeFevre. He snatched up his hat and pair of sabres in a leather case. At the door of Nita's room, he hesitated. Steeling himself, he stepped inside and gazed down upon the face of the woman he loved. Even in her drugged sleep, she tossed and strained against her bonds. Her face was awry. He bent over her, touched his lips to her forehead, then whirled and was gone. It came over him that this was goodbye. There was small chance that he would survive the meeting with LeFevre. But one thing he swore. LeFevre should die!

125

LeFevre toppled into space and Wentworth's sabre sunk into his second assailant!

CHAPTER 9
DEATH'S BRIGHT BLADE

W ENTWORTH HAD parked his Hispano road-ster at the curb before the apartment house. He flung swiftly to the seat, kicked the motor to life and roared up Fifth Avenue with a wide open engine. Within three blocks, he was doing seventy miles an hour, ignoring traffic lights on the deserted streets of dawn. It would be minutes before police surveillance could pick up his trail, and in that time LeFevre must make contact.

Reaching Fortieth Street, Wentworth cut his speed a little and in the Fifties, he caught sight of a limousine that swung out of a cross street and spurted to overtake him. Alertly, he slowed the Hispano. This might be LeFevre ready for the duel, and it might be LeFevre's men with submachine guns! He saw that there was only one man in the car, a chauffeur. Seeing that Wentworth's eyes were on him, the man signaled.

The transfer was made in two seconds and the Hispano was left at the curb Wentworth was aware of roaring police cars a dozen blocks behind, but they were left immediately as the limousine whirled from Fifth Avenue and executed a series of quick doubles on its own trail. Five minutes later, it drew to a halt before a high building in the East Thirties. The chauffeur had not spoken and now he gestured toward an alleyway that led toward the building's rear. Wentworth grimly signed for him to lead the way, and loosened a sabre in its case. But no treachery became apparent. They entered an elevator that lifted swiftly. Wentworth counted the floors, and it was the eighteenth at which they stopped. From there, a short flight of stairs led to the roof and once more Wentworth motioned the chauffeur forward.

The man flashed him a smile as he obeyed, threw the door at the top of the steps wide and stood to one side in plain view. Against the far parapet of the roof, LeFevre leaned with folded arms. No one else was in sight, but Wentworth stepped cautiously through the doorway, whirled on his heel to sweep the roof in a single comprehensive glance. Except for LeFevre and the chauffeur, it was empty. Wentworth was puzzled, but not deceived. He knew that the Frenchman would not risk his life in this way without stauncher support than this single chauffeur. But it was true also that only one man with a gun was enough to turn the tables at any point of the struggle....

LeFevre took two strides forward and bowed, his face grave "That was clever of you, *m'sieur*, racing away from the police before they could begin surveillance. I perceive that you are in a hurry?"

Wentworth slipped out of his coat, tossed his hat after it to the roof. He wore no tie, his sleeves were rolled up and his feet were encased in light-weight, rubber-soled shoes. His gaze met LeFevre's levelly, without heat, but with a cold determination that brought a smile to LeFevre's lips.

"So?" he said softly. He threw aside his own coat, squatted once to loosen his trousers about the knees and flexed his wrist. "I see you have brought your own sabre, *m'sieur*. If they are the sabres that I did not take... Ah, perfect! We shall use them!"

Wentworth coldly offered the sabres over his forearm, hilt first, tossed the other into the air and caught it. He whipped it swishing through the air, came to rest in an easy guard.

"Ready, LeFevre!" His voice rang like steel.

The Frenchman put his left hand on his hip, lifted the point of the sabre until it pointed at Wentworth's eyes and nodded briefly.

"Tout prêt!" he cried softly. "All ready!"

INSTANTLY, WENTWORTH attacked. There was no caution in his veins this morning, and room only for death. If he could strike swiftly and fatally, he might upset LeFevre's plans....

LeFevre retreated three swift paces before the clanging lash of Wentworth's blade, then made a stand, parrying with a contained conservatism of movement that bespoke entire mastery of sabre fighting. Wentworth beat at the head, changed the blow to a thrust with the edge for the throat, cut backhand as he withdrew. And all three blows were warded almost without effort.

Instantly, LeFevre launched his own attack. He was too small for a force assault, whatever the strength of his wrist and arm, but his sabre moved with the speed of a foil.

Wentworth retreated, got his back to the parapet, with LeFevre before him, and suddenly he laughed aloud. It was a fierce mocking sound, filled with a bitter triumph. The roof had been empty except for the two duelists and the chauffeur. Now there were at least a half dozen men about the kiosk, watching the swift play of the sabres. One of them had a familiar look, but

Wentworth could not place the man exactly. He was tall, with a lithe grace of movement that was almost sinister. He kept to the background, and the brim of a wide hat shielded his face.

"Your reinforcements have arrived, LeFevre!" Wentworth cried. "Be brave for them!" His blade became a flail of light. The hammer of the steel rang and rang again and, slowly, lips twisting in venomous snarl, LeFevre retreated. His sabre guarded perfectly, but twice he was almost too slow for the twirling speed of the attack. With the abruptness of a striking snake, Wentworth stopped slashing and thrust. His point struck hard and true to LeFevre's breast, driving him backward. The sabre bent almost double under the strain of the thrust, but its point did not penetrate. With a cry of rage, Wentworth renewed his slashing attack.

"Mail!" he shouted. "Dog of a coward, you wear a shirt of mail in a duel! It won't save you! Nothing can save you…!"

In his anger, Wentworth had turned his back toward the other men crowded on the roof. Instantly, he realized his danger and sought to retreat. He was too late. Something tripped him and he pitched heavily to the roof on his back. He was instantly on a knee, but he was too late to block completely LeFevre's furious lunge. The point took Wentworth high on the shoulder near the throat, ripped through flesh and tore loose again. Before LeFevre could strike again, Wentworth's blade, on his chest again, had driven him backward and Wentworth was on his feet once more.

His wound was a burning knife in his shoulder and he could feel the warm wash of blood over chest and back. He was facing his enemies again. LeFevre lashing at him almost toe to toe. It had been the chauffeur who tripped him with a long pole, he saw. Two of the men held guns. Truly, the Spider would not be allowed to escape! Wentworth saw those things. He felt the weakness of his draining blood, and he threw back his head and *laughed!*

Even LeFevre wavered before that touch of madness. An unwilling admiration sprang into his eyes. A man who could laugh in the face of certain death! Wentworth lunged again savagely, the vehemence of his sword brushing aside the French-man's guard. He aimed for the throat, but the touch of the parry had been enough to divert his blade and once more the point hit strongly against the mail shirt. Its point penetrated a little way, the blade bent double to the hilt and snapped clean near the hilt! LeFEVRE STAGGERED back, his sabre drooping, but he laughed! "Do you think even killing me would save you, pig?" LeFevre cried. "It shall not save you!" He tossed his sword to another man. "Finish the dog, but not yet, not until I have told him what is going to happen to his mistress and to these people he loved so, the people of America…" He thrust his angry, writhing face forward. "This afternoon, my fool, we drive a whole city mad! Do you understan'? We drive a whole city mad! Those we make insane yesterday? Jus' an experimen', a proof to our employer that we can do what we say. Now, in a little while we drive this whole city mad so that this man will no more have a rival factory. When we drive these men mad they will destroy the factory, perhap' destroy his rival too.

"*Comprenes?* This woman of yours?" LeFevre rocked with his laughter. "She will be forever… *foue!* Now, *mes enfants*, kill him!"

Other men rushed forward.

"Not with guns, you fools," a man shouted. "He must be killed with the sword!" Anger surged hot in Wentworth's throat. He knew abruptly that the man who shouted was the man behind the scenes! This was the Master of the Insanity Drug, the one who directed LeFevre's efforts. A thought flashed into his brain, he heard confirmation of his guess, heard the man berating LeFevre with scorn harsh in his voice.

"Even with a coat of mail under your shirt, you can't beat him," the man said. "You call yourself a great swordsman!"

Wentworth leaned against the parapet, the broken sabre still in his hand. His guns were under his shirt, but his left arm was useless, the muscles slashed by LeFevre's blow. If he dropped his sabre to get to an automatic... But it was useless. There were two guns on him and one of the men had caught up LeFevre's sabre. Best to oppose the sword. They wanted to kill him in that way. It would be so many more minutes of life, so many more minutes when something might intervene... *Something?* What could happen, unless he gave a warning in some way? He had deliberately thrown the police off his trail. He stared at LeFevre and suddenly, again, he laughed. A warning? He had an inspiration!

With nothing more than that laughter, Wentworth hurled himself upon the man with the sword, stabbing at him viciously with his broken blade. The man was trained in the sabre somewhat, it was clear. He fell back on defense, retreated... Abruptly, Wentworth dropped the pretense of dueling and sprang on LeFevre. With the Frenchman in his arms; he sprang to the crest of the parapet.

"Shoot me!" he cried. "Shoot me, and LeFevre falls to his death! Nineteen stories to his death!"

The gunmen let their weapons fall, but the man with the sabre sprang forward, blade snaking out to stab. Wentworth's lips twisted up from his teeth. He felt LeFevre's feet drumming at his shins, his hands reaching backward to hammer at his body. This squirming thing was the creature who had brought so much horror to humanity, who had destroyed Nita's soul, wrecked the lives of so many others. This man…!

The sword cut at Wentworth's legs. With a curse, he released his hold on LeFevre, leaped to the roof again, whirled with his broken sword on guard. LeFevre teetered on the parapet, screaming, his arms wind-milling in frightened, panic circles. A man leaped forward to help him and his hands brushed LeFevre's legs. It was all that was needed. LeFevre toppled out into space. His horrified scream rose in frantic terror, died off brokenly into distance. The man with the sabre stood frozen with shock and Wentworth sprang forward. Here was no horror for him. Here was triumph! And LeFevre, whose screams Wentworth had counted on to summon help, would guide the police in still another way when his body shattered on the street below. **THE BROKEN** blade of Wentworth's sword streaked home with his weight behind it, and the man who took that thrust did not scream. He reeled backward, pawing at his torn throat and Wentworth snatched the undamaged sabre, vaulted over the parapet and crouched on the narrow ledge that circled the roof just outside the low railing. If he could hold out for a few moments, a few scant minutes, help would be here. Those screams and that crashing fall assured that. He drew an automatic, fired a salvo of shots into the air, skimming chips from the parapet.

"Let him go!" shouted the voice, which Wentworth recognized as the leader's. "Let him go! The police will trap us here."

Rage closed Wentworth's throat. He sprang erect, gun ready to smash death into the fleeing leader and he looked into the blazing muzzles of three guns. He pitched backward, only saved himself from that deadly plunge by catching the edge of the parapet, dropping his gun. He had taken lead somewhere in his body. He recognized the sledge hammer blow, that numbing attack of pain. But they must not know; those killers must not know.

Wentworth screamed. He lifted his voice in just such frantic terror as LeFevre had voiced on that last wild plunge and, with a skill for which he found the stamina somewhere in his great soul, he made that sound seem to fade downward into distance. He heard a voice shout, "All right. Hurry! He's gone. Hurry, fools, the police. *Les flicks…!*

Darkness closed in on Wentworth's soul.

CHAPTER 10
A CITY IS DOOMED

D EEP IN Wentworth's subconscious being he felt an urgency, a pressing *need* to come back to life. Something that was overwhelmingly important; that meant more than life or death.

"Quiet, man," a voice ordered. "Don't try to talk!"

Wentworth rolled his head, burst out of the shrouds of darkness and found himself gazing into Kirkpatrick's saturnine face.

"Back to my apartment," Wentworth whispered. "Phone there… at once."

Kirkpatrick soothed him, "Yes, yes, we will. It's all right, Dick. LeFevre is dead."

Wentworth's voice broke loose, shouting. "All right, hell! LeFevre is just an underling! A whole city is to be destroyed this afternoon. A whole city, Kirk! He taunted me with it when he thought I was done for.…"

Kirkpatrick stared intently into Wentworth's face, and his own gaze hardened. "I thought you were delirious," he explained sharply. "God forgive me! What city, Dick?"

Wentworth rolled his head. He forced himself up from the bed. "I don't know!" he cried. "I don't know. He didn't say. Will you get my home on the telephone?"

Kirkpatrick sprang from the bedside and Wentworth realized that he was in a hospital and that stiff bandages were about his shoulder and side. He thrust himself to his feet, stood swaying. A nurse looked in, came forward with outstretched, soothing hands.

"Get my clothes!" Wentworth shouted at her. "Get my clothes, and don't think the internes can get me back in bed!"

A man came in behind the nurse and Wentworth waited until he was quite near and struck with the neatness and the timing that always marked his actions. The interne stiffened and pitched forward across the bed, out cold, and Kirkpatrick came back into the room, followed by a nurse with a portable telephone.

"Dick!" Kirkpatrick cried. "Man, you can't do this! You're badly wounded!"

Wentworth laughed at him. "Plug in that phone, nurse." His eyes held Kirkpatrick's. "What the hell difference do wounds make? What time is it?"

Kirkpatrick looked at his wrist watch. "Almost noon. Dick, you will have to get back in bed."

Wentworth snatched the phone from the nurse's hands. "Kirk, get my clothes," he commanded shortly. "Hello, all right, Jaffrey, has James phoned in? From New Brunswick, New Jersey? All right, I'll phone from there. Listen, tell him again, he must not interfere with that girl on any count. A thousand souls depend on it? All right, be sure you make him understand…" He stared straight before him, listening, his hands white on the telephone, his lean, brown face drawn taut with lines of suffering. There was a will and a fury about him that would not be denied. Kirkpatrick, staring into his face, spoke shortly to a nurse and she went away to get clothing. Wentworth said heavily, "Thanks." He hung up, the nurse came back with the clothes and he began to throw them on before she had closed the door. Kirkpatrick came to be assistance because of that wounded left arm.

"Would you mind telling me what's happening" he demanded. "How's Nita?"

"Don't mention her again!" Wentworth shouted. "Come on!" He started for the door, reeled and collided with the wall. He leaned there for a moment, panting, sweat forming in big

137

drops on his forehead. Then he thrust away from the wall and made the door. There was a policeman at the door and Wentworth took his gun from his holster. When the man would have interfered, Kirkpatrick nodded to him. Gun in hand, Wentworth staggered along the hall. His face was frozen into a frowning mold. His lips moved, soundlessly. He was saying over and over, "I must not think about Nita. I must not think about Nita." He was forming the words very carefully, so that he would be sure to understand them.

THERE WAS a doctor and a nurse on the elevator. They stared at Wentworth and the doctor's hand went quietly to his pocket, came out with a syringe wrapped in an antiseptic pad. Kirkpatrick seized his wrist, but the man shook his head.

"Heart stimulant," he said. "I had it for an emergency that didn't develop. He needs it."

Wentworth frowned at him, as if he heard the words with an effort. His lips were still moving. "All right," he said, "but if it's a trick, I'll kill you when I recover consciousness." Wentworth uttered the words flatly, without emphasis, but the doctor paled.

"It's no trick," he whispered. He stammered, saying it.

He injected the contents of the needle into Wentworth's throat and when Wentworth left the elevator, he walked a little more steadily. He gripped Kirkpatrick's wrist with hard fingers.

"Margie Huron will go to Charlton," he said. "James is following her."

Kirkpatrick laid his hand over Wentworth's. His face was sagging with disappointment. "There's no need for you to go. We've tried that before...."

Wentworth twisted his head about and grinned derisively into Kirkpatrick's face.

"This time it will work," he said, "Margie's taking James to Charlton's hideout."

"She's taking him?" Kirkpatrick did not appear to understand. "You mean that she's leading him, deliberately...?"

Wentworth's grin wouldn't come off, but there was no mirth in it at all. "She loves Charlton," he said, "so she's taking Detective Jesse James to his hideout. She loves James, too."

Kirkpatrick settled back in the rear of a powerful police sedan. "New Brunswick, New Jersey," he said. "Use the siren and travel as fast as you can!" The driver didn't often get orders like that from Kirkpatrick. He liked to drive fast. The sedan jumped away from the curb, the siren shrieked and it took the first corner westward leaning far over. Kirkpatrick looked again at Wentworth. His eyes were harassed, worried.

"I'm going to sleep until we reach New Brunswick," Wentworth said. His lips spoke out loud the words he had been saying in his mind, "I will not think about Nita." He rested his head against the cushions and presently, despite the lurching speed, the whooping glee of the siren, he slept. Miles roared under the whining tires. Kirkpatrick sat rigidly, and the frown stayed on his forehead. What Wentworth said didn't make sense, but he was accustomed to follow where Wentworth led... A whole city to be destroyed, an industrial city destroyed, by insanity. Through the miles, a hard tension crept into his muscles. His breath came in long sighs. Wentworth had to be right. He had to be… Why did he keep whispering about Nita, that he must not think of her?

New Brunswick was a weary distance. Wentworth lifted his head as they rolled into its outskirts. "Phone my house, Kirk," he asked quietly. "Ask Jaffrey about James' call. Trying to save my strength…!"

Kirkpatrick came back. "Trenton," he yelled at the driver. The car's tires spun on the gravel, took hold on concrete and jerked it forward with mounting speed. Wentworth looked at him, a question in his eyes. Kirkpatrick's lips twitched.

"There's no change in Nita's condition," he said.

"No change?" Wentworth whispered. "No change…!"

A MOTORCYCLE policeman spurted up beside the sedan with a blasting whistle. Kirkpatrick leaned from the window, shouting; and after that the motorcycle sirened a way through traffic and their speed mounted, seventy-five, eighty, eighty-five….

Kirkpatrick leaned toward Wentworth, "I told the New Brunswick operator to have Trenton get through to your house on one of your wires and hold it open. We'll save time…."

Wentworth nodded, but he did not seem to hear. His lips did not move. His eyes were narrowed with pain. He stared straight ahead. At Trenton, Kirkpatrick hurled from the car without a word. The motorcycle cop dropped back and peered into the back.

"Some time!" he grinned. "You boys must be in a hurry."

Wentworth did not answer him, and the cop's grin faded. His face got a little white. He whispered to the police chauffeur. Kirkpatrick sprang back into the car and the motorcycle sputtered ahead.

"It's Spensertown," he said. His voice sounded dead. Spensertown had miles on miles of explosives factories. There were great storage fields full of explosives and more than twelve thousand humans worked in them. There was a grayness about Kirkpatrick's mouth.

"Spensertown!" he said. "They were there an hour a ago."

A hundred thousand tons of explosive and madmen loose among them. Wentworth shook his head, pressed the heel of his hand to his forehead.

"Still no change," he said.

The bridge over the Delaware thumped past under the wheels, cars skittered to the side out of their screaming path. Woods and houses blurred past. There were many turns and the tires screamed, the men in the car swayed to one side, then to the other.

"I have a street address," Kirkpatrick said dully, "but I'm afraid we'll be too late. It was an hour ago."

Wentworth reached under his coat and got out the police revolver he had tucked into his belt. He thumbed open the gate. "I wish that cop hadn't been so careful. Only five bullets."

Kirkpatrick dug a handful out of his packet. They cut the siren when they entered Spensertown, and that cut their speed. It was still enough to make them dry-skid corners. Finally the car cut to the curb.

"A block down, half a block to the left," the motorcycle cop told them. "Shall I get some help?"

Wentworth nodded. "Get out the reserves, but keep them quiet. They're to wait for the signal of a shot…" He walked very erectly down the center of the pavement. Kirkpatrick stalked at his elbow. They kept their hands in their pockets on guns.

"What are your plans?" Kirkpatrick asked.

Wentworth's lips moved in a little smile. "I'm going in," he said. Kirkpatrick opened his mouth, but didn't say anything. His mouth closed thinly and he walked steadily along beside Wentworth. When they came to the address that had been given him, Wentworth walked up the short sidewalk, to the porch of the house. The door swung open and there were five men with guns, a sawed-off shotgun, a submachine gun. The men grinned.

"We've been expecting you," one of them said.

"A trap," Kirkpatrick whispered.

Wentworth ignored him and ignored the men. He walked through them like an automaton and they gave way before him. In the room beyond the hall, Ricey Charlton sat at ease in a lounge chair. Margie Huron sat on the edge of hers. Detective Jesse James was tied, hand and foot. Charlton nodded pleasantly, his angular, dark face very pleased. He grinned when men mauled Wentworth and Kirkpatrick in taking their guns away.

"You're just in time," he said. "I've arranged a little show for your benefit. This little button—" he indicated a telegraph instrument on the table beside him—"will cause a little explosion at the bottom of the city reservoir. It will hardly cause a ripple at the top, but it will release enough drugs into the city water-supply to make everybody in it completely insane in a matter of a few hours, depending on how soon each one takes a drink. Wentworth, you will press this button for me."

WENTWORTH LOOKED into his face, unsmiling. He looked at Margie Huron. "Nita's condition is unchanged," he called to her slowly. "It's after one o'clock. Quite a bit after noon."

Margie started to her feet. Wentworth faced Charlton. "I will not press the button," he stated flatly.

Charlton nodded pleasantly, and a man took out a knife and pressed it to Kirkpatrick's throat just over the carotid artery.

"It takes two minutes to bleed to death from a cut carotid," Charlton explained with grisly humor.

Wentworth shook his head, his face wooden. "I will not press the button," he said.

Charlton snapped to his feet. He recognized the stony indifference in Wentworth's face. At his sign, the knife was taken from Kirkpatrick's throat and pressed to that of Wentworth.

"I don't care especially about killing Kirkpatrick," Charlton said pleasantly, "But I'll take especial delight in ridding the world, and myself, of you, Wentworth. But I won't kill you. The tip of that knife has the insanity drug upon it. In your throat, that way, it will make you permanently insane, just as we made your woman." Wentworth struck Charlton with an economy of motion that almost hid the powerful blow. Charlton picked himself up from the floor, took the knife and pressed the point against Wentworth's left eye. A man held each of Wentworth's arms. Charlton laughed.

"Think, Wentworth, think," he whispered. "It is the last time you will have the power to think." He tensed his shoulder, his face hardened....

From her seat, Margie Huron spoke suddenly, rapidly. "You can't do it, Charlie. You can't. He could have given me the drug and he didn't do it. And he had more reason to do it than you did. You gave the drug to his sweetheart. Mr. Wentworth, I didn't know that. I swear to you that I didn't. I thought it was LeFevre..." She got to her feet, laid her hand on Charlton's arm. "Please, Charlie, for my sake...?"

Charlton struck Margie heavily across the face and the blow flung her to the floor. She lay there, panting, her eyes on Charlton's face. There was no anger there, no hurt, only decision. Detective James was cursing violently. Kirkpatrick was held helpless, and Wentworth merely stared straight into Charlton's face.

"That was like you, Charlton," he said, "but I think it is the last time you'll strike your sister. Look at her."

Charlton whipped about. He screamed, "For God's sake, Margie...!" He choked, pressing his hands to his stomach where the bullet the girl fired had struck. He pitched forward on his face. Margie Huron got slowly to her feet, her face very white.

"Every mother's son of you put down your guns," she said, and there was a quality in her voice that was very like Charlton's. Guns thumped to the floor. "Get out," she ordered, *"Get out!"*

There was the shuffling of feet as men tramped from the room. Margie held very rigidly to her pose behind the gun until the last of them was gone, then she crumpled. She hadn't fainted, but the starch had gone out of her. She caught up Charlton's head and cradled it in her arms as she had once held Detective James.

"Charlie," she whimpered. "Oh, Charlie, I had to do it! It was the only way I could save your immortal soul!"

Charlton's face was wrinkled with pain. He reached up and slapped Margie across the mouth. He shuddered and collapsed. "It wasn't… the last… time!" he whispered triumphantly. He died with his eyes on Wentworth's. Off somewhere in the building, a telephone bell rang, quit, rang again. It kept that up.

WENTWORTH SMILED gently on Margie Huron. "I'm sorry, Margie," he whispered, "but it was your soul that had to be saved. You had to realize that your brother was all bad, that you could never save him, no matter how hard you tried, and I know you have tried. It was better that you do it, rather than anyone else; rather than Jesse James, whom you love."

Margie bowed her head into her hands and began to cry. Wentworth nodded. That was all right then. She could cry. The telephone bell was still ringing.

Wentworth bent over and picked up the knife that Charlton had held. With it, he cut Detective James' bonds. A stunned look was in James' eyes.

"How did you know it was her brother?" he whispered. "How do you know she loves me?"

"No girl like Margie could love two men the same way at the same time, James," Wentworth told him quietly. "Her love is too deep for fickleness. And she loved you. Anybody else but a blind fool like you would have known that. Go to her, James, boy"

He turned away. The telephone bell stopped ringing and presently Kirkpatrick's voice rang through the house. "Dick, Dick, man! Come to the phone." That voice reached somewhere into the depths of Wentworth's soul and stirred something that he had thought was dead. It stirred hope. He stumbled, running towards Kirkpatrick. His hands trembled as he reached for the phone. The voice over the wire....

Wentworth sank down on his knees, feeling the tears roll down his cheeks, feeling happiness burst its bonds within him.

"Nita," he whispered. "Nita… Thank God!"

It was her voice over the wire. "I suppose God did have something to do with it, Dick," she was saying, "but this ugly, red-headed galoot we call a doctor was God's little angel, I guess. He found… the antidote."